Dam Diligent

Dam Diligent

Dam Diligent
(BOOK ONE)

IAN TRAFFORD WALKER

PARTRIDGE
A Penguin Random House Company

Print information available on the last page.

To order additional copies of this book, contact
Toll Free 800 101 2657 (Singapore)
Toll Free 1 800 81 7340 (Malaysia)
orders.singapore@partridgepublishing.com

www.partridgepublishing.com/singapore

Contents

This book is dedicated to my parents

Edith Jean Walker and Ralph Trafford Walker

Both of whom helped produce

Dam Diligent

Introduction

Dam Diligent grew up in a cave forty feet above the sea. The cave looked out over the ocean and witnessed the passing of a city's commerce while he caught fish, surfed and grew vegetables.

He would spend his days writing and painting and there was no man happier than he.

As time grew long, the same as his teeth, he began to hunger for the wider world and the embellishment of his genes.

Now after a thousand shipwrecks, he finds himself stranded in the wild trees being blown by the attitudes of the civilizing whim of the weather.

This collection of stories retrace some of his and other's steps, be they tepid or wayward - that is for the reader's spleen to fathom.

May Dam live on in the joyous hearts of those who refuse to grow up and suffer the soliloquies of times wretched claws.

ITW

2015

Dam's Damn Skateboards

When Dam was a young boy he went to a school in the city which was all covered in asphalt. It was black and hard and horrible. There were few places where the real ground emerged. In those places rocks, trees and small patches of grass had been left around the edges where they clung desperately like sea-weeds to avoid the black hot desert wash.

Dam was young when he received his first pair of roller skates. His parents gave them to him for his birthday. Perhaps it was because they lived on a steep hill or they knew Dam's school playground was full of lumps and humps and generally smooth, just made for skating!

Dam practiced at home until he thought he was pretty good. One day he packed his school lunch and put his skates on his feet. No more walking on footpaths for Dam. He was off down the middle of the bitumen road. He had his own method of transport.

He was early to school that day and by the time the morning bell rang for assembly crowds of children were running through the playground screaming with excitement chasing Dam who stood tall on his skates.

Dam walked up the stairs to his class with them on. He tied them up and hang them on a hook with his bag. Dam caused quite a stir in the playground that day. Three girls fell trying to catch up to the huge crowd which was practically the whole school, chasing him!

People in front were pushing Dam as he crouched down with his arms around his knees! They would push him up the hill and then down until

1

Dam was going much faster than they. He would then go over a slight bump jumping high in the air to stop suddenly near the gate.

Two boys fell and grazed their knees and two others ran into each other hurting both their noses. The only person not injured and not exhausted from running was Dam. At the end of the day he put his skates on and sailed off down the road home.

The next day at school Dam was told to take his skates home as they were dangerous.

At break time he had to leave them tied up on the hook. He still used them to and from school though.

Months later he became bored with his skates and decided to cut one of them in half and put a piece of wood on the top of the four wheels. That way there was less to carry and he could place his school bag on the wood and sit on it and go along!

He found he could use the skateboard like a scooter and push it along with the other foot. Dam was very pleased with his invention. Everybody was interested and said,

"What's that?" But it wasn't enough, Dam cut the board in half and hinged the two halves together so he could fit it in his school bag. There was no room for books in there!

People would point and laugh to see Dam speeding down the footpath on his suitcase with his feet out the sides for steering and brakes.

He found he could turn a little by leaning from side to side. This was difficult as often the suitcase would slip off and more than once Dam had to bail out on the grass or leap into an overhanging tree to escape bad injury.

Now Dam being diligent had another idea and made another skateboard out of his other skate. This he strapped to his other foot. Dam remembered one time well as he had no brakes to stop himself. How Dam escaped serious injury was a mystery! But once he overtook a truck which was going down the hill half a kilometre from the bottom. The driver of the truck leaned forward, he could not believe his eyes.

Dam oiled his wheels and developed a device for keeping stones from jamming under the front wheels because small stones which jammed suddenly made a very good break which would not stop Dam who kept on going!

But Dam being Dam had an idea to stop them jamming. He had often ended up draped over somebody's garden fence. Dogs were generally quite terrified of him.

He remembered often having to use other objects as brakes. Such as the time when a small white dog saw him coming forty meters away. Dam didn't expect to go anywhere near the dog which was standing in front of a garage door but he was going faster than running when a tiny stone made the left skateboard stop instantly. This spun Dam right around! Somehow he managed to re-land the board, which was strapped onto his foot, the other board took off with Dam's leg still on it! He seemed to leave his left leg behind and braced himself for a sore bottom when miraculously the other board touched down just as he saw a small white blur and then the great blank space of the garage door!

"Bang!" there was a huge noise like thunder. Dam hit the door fair and square with his arms outstretched and the two skateboards stuck straight through it so he was stuck standing there! People began to emerge from houses everywhere to see what the great noise was! After a little while Dam felt himself rising as somebody opened the door from inside! Dam was hidden and squashed on the roof!

"Oh!" said the man, "there's a man on the door!"

Soon other people appeared with skateboards in other countries.

Big companies were making high quality skateboards and Dam wanted four. Why he wanted four nobody knew not even his parents. To make money he went around all his friends at school both young and old and asked if he could have a very small amount of money, so small it did not matter to them.

He even went and collected the afternoon newspapers which the paper delivery man had thrown in people's driveways and took them to the front door of the houses and asked for a tiny amount of money for bringing it to the door! One old person laughed and said she could get it herself for nothing!

Dam put the paper back in a tree where she couldn't reach it. But sometime later he went back and took it up to her front door and left it on the front step.

Soon Dam had enough saved up and bought two boards. His parents knew he was up to something when he attached both of them to his knees. It wasn't long before Dam had his four boards and these other two he strapped to his elbows. Now he had six skateboards!

With much practice Dam could do cartwheels down the road at sixty kilometres an hour upside down! He made the boards connect together at the sides as well as the front and rear. This cart or trolley could then be steered from the front with a piece of string and was good for helping his mother with the shopping.

Dam installed small breaks on the rear wheels. They were activated by a small lever which worked when he put weight on it. This way Dam could take up to five friends with him, one on each board tied on behind. This was great fun as they found they could move along flat ground simply by moving from side to side like a long fish. When they picked up speed it was dangerous and Dam was asked to stand on the rear board. He couldn't understand why they didn't use the brakes? He left his friends hanging in trees!

However Dam liked best of all to use his skateboards on his elbows and knees. He was becoming a familiar figure around the shops. One had to be quick to see him though as he was always travelling so fast. And there wasn't much to see of him anyway as he was kneeling down and only half his size.

His head was so low to the ground and his rear end was thrust up in the air - he didn't look very talkative or sociable.

He was always on the move. He liked doing things efficiently he was Dam Diligent. Some people thought he was wheely clever.

He bought himself a crash helmet and wore a leather jacket. When he stood up and walked along he sounded like a knight in jangling armour.

Generally he didn't like walking and spent his days off school doing tricks on the side of the road. Dam soon grew tired of his small boards and began to dream about making a limousine board, a big long one, one he could walk up and down on. However when he made that he soon grew board with it too and was always thinking of new things to add to it.

Dam being the nut and axle that he was, decided to put some wings on his extra-long skate board. But first he realised some speed would be necessary. Dam set about reinventing the wheel. He made special wheel-hubs with a slight camber and set a spring in between the two sets of axles so that one had to bob up and down to make the contraption go along. Next he designed the wings.

Dam reckoned that if his weight could make the board go forward then why couldn't he make the skateboard go up in the air? He set about experimenting with green bendy sticks and a few bits of string and a few funny levers before he was ready. There was one problem and that was that Dam had to push down with his arms as well as jump up and down to make the wings flap and the skateboard move. He wondered about the engineering for a while and decided to test it out to get a better understanding of the dynamics involved.

The day he chose for the test run was slightly windy - blowing up the big hill, just right! Dam put his crash helmet on and modified a beach umbrella as a parachute. He packed his board and wings under his arm and with a beach umbrella under his arm walked up to the top of the hill. As he walked he collected a crowd of little followers.

When Dam reached the top the wind had become quite strong. So strong that he had difficulty fixing the wings as each one was two meters long. They were light and strong, he had made them out of paper and light wood.

Dam was ready. With one foot on the road and the other on his board he lowered the visor of the helmet and lifted his other leg. Just then there was a strong gust of wind and rather than move forward he was thrown sideways and had to get two friends to hold his wings. With his beach umbrella between his legs sticking out backwards and holding the release string, he slowly moved forward. But Dam did not move he stayed quite still!

Dam put his arms behind him as some of the children watching came forward and gave him a push. The wind died a little and more children stepped forward to help push. Dam was soon moving fast down the hill. The children were screaming and squealing with delight as they ran after him. Then Dam began furiously to work his springy board and bob up and down and move his arms to gather speed.

He soon left the children far behind and then for an instant he was airborne! Just as he was approaching the cross-roads near the bottom of the hill a bus appeared right in the middle of the road!

It all happened too quickly for Dam to remember anything. He woke up next to a swimming pool with a rose in his mouth, surrounded by many people.

"Oh you were so lucky!" said one person.

"Gave me such a fright!" said another.

Dam lay half in the water and half out with his parachute open, it had probably saved his life. He was staring at the sky when a young girl stepped forward and said,

"You again, you're the person who smashed into my mother's garage door. You gave her a hell of a fright! And that's my rose!" she said bending down.

"I was just about to sniff that!" Dam suddenly focused on her face as she came close, she was beautiful and had a pink face or was he seeing her through the petals of the rose? She reached down and wrenched it from his lips, cutting his lip slightly and stormed back onto the bus.

Apparently Dam had flown straight through the windows of the bus, collecting the rose in his mouth on the way. He had gone clean over the road then over a fence and landed in somebody's swimming pool where his parachute had finally opened! His skateboard was still sticking in the side of the bus!

At least nobody was hurt and Dam had needed a bath anyway! His beautiful wings were all broken and torn. He took them over to a garbage bin and threw them in. He wrapped up the wet umbrella and put his wet helmet back on his head. He said he was very sorry to the bus driver and would pay for the hole in the bus. And as the wind blew chilly down his back, Dam took his skateboard and walked back up the hill to home.

Dam and the Echidna

Dam stepped on the bus, he was wearing his pet echidna on his head, it looked like the new hairstyle and Dam hoped nobody would notice its long nose in front of his forehead. He paid his fare but before any change was given Echi, as the echidna was called, stuck out his long sticky tongue and mopped up a handful of gold coins from the till. Luckily the driver was looking in the rear vision mirror at the time and didn't see, however the coins all bounced and fell onto the floor.

Dam and the driver began to pick them up but some of them rolled down the stairs. After sometime Dam stood up and walked inside smiling at a good looking lady as he did. He found a seat at the back of the bus and pretended to scratch his head but he was really feeling for Echi's claws which usually gripped Dam's ears.

He was gone! Dam jumped up and felt his head all over, then he looked out the back of the bus to see if Echi had been left behind. No Echi was on the bus. Dam sat down again and let out a shriek for he sat on Echi whose spines were very sharp. Some people turned around and Dam's bald patch was soon hidden again with Echi's warm belly.

Presently a lady came and sat in the seat in front of Dam, she had a great mass of wavy purple hair. Dam thought nothing of it and began to read his newspaper. But the purple hair suddenly fell into his newspaper as Echi had secured it with his sticky tongue and pulled it off the woman's head!

Not knowing what to do, Dam gently placed it back on her head but his fingers touched the sticky part and he could not release them.

The woman suddenly reached up and felt her hair but came upon Dam's hands wriggling and trying to get free! The woman's wig came off again as Dam's other hand tried to help his fingers get free but to the woman it looked like Dam was mangling her wig! With a loud shriek and swing of her arm she launched her hand-bag at Dam's head. Echi was not impressed and unfortunately became impaled on the woman's hand-bag. Dam was showing his bald patch again and poor Echi was being hurled about the bus!

Dam's bald patch has never been the same since and he never goes on public transport with his pet Echidna anymore!

Dam Learns How to Drive

When Dam was a lot younger he longed to take ladies out driving in the country side.

To this end he'd dyed his hair an unusual colour in the hope of attracting them. He also decided to buy a car and learn how to drive.

"Would you like to come driving with me?" he would say to himself in his most eloquent language. "A Sunday drive in the country?"

"Ah," said Dam as he stared in the mirror, "these blond locks will have them swarming in!"

He liked to dress in a blue suit with a pink bow-tie. He was young and naïve and thought he was attractive.

Dam had a little bit of money scraped up for a car so he bought a foreign one with a strange name he couldn't pronounce. The car looked good and so did he, the only thing he needed was a license. He booked himself in at a reputable driving school and stood beside his brand new red car dressed in his brand new blue suit and pink bow-tie and waited for the driving instructor to arrive.

She came right on time.

Oh and Dam thought she was beautiful! She had a massive amount of bright red frizzy hair almost the same colour as Dam's car and her dress was vivid red too!

"What luck!" thought Dam.

"Sit beside me," she said as he nervously bent his knees which crackled like fire-crackers as he moved.

"Is this your first time?" she asked. He looked across at her but all he could see was an exploding mass of red hair.

"Yes," he replied in a small voice.

"Okay I'll run through the controls."

Unfortunately Dam didn't hear a thing, he was overcome by her perfume.

"Don't press on that or you'll hit a bridge" she was saying pointing at the ejector button. "I've never seen one of those before….Now the car is in automatic so you don't have to clutch."

"Clutch, clutch what?" Dam repeated not knowing what she meant.

"Mirrors and safety-belt and first gear."

Dam was suddenly normal and strapped in. He started the car. The engine sounded like an aeroplane idling and suddenly the car lifted slightly.

Dam wondered if it might rise in the air.

"Oh this is easy," he thought as he drew out from the curb.

"You've driven before?" the lady asked.

"No," said Dam and added "it's your wonderful teaching."

"Ha," she said studying his strange blond hair.

Dam was driving quite well for his first time. They were in three lanes of traffic going down a hill, the car speeded up a little.

"Would you like to come for a Sunday drive with me?" said Dam exhaling perfume.

"What?" said the lady. Dam was about to speak again when she suddenly said,

"What do you call three blonds in a row?"

"I beg your pardon" said Dam.

The lady then said "A wind tunnel."

"Eh?" said Dam.

"Why did the blond climb a glass wall?"

"I don't know" he said, cracking his knees.

"To see what was on the other side. Ha ha ha ha." The woman's laugh sounded like a diesel engine starting up!

The hill grew steeper and her perfume was beginning to make Dam feel sick.

Then without warning the car was going too fast. The woman called,

"Brake! brake!" and thrust her great red-stockinged leg across in front of him jabbing his crackly knees as she tried to find the brake. She was also grabbing at the wheel!

Dam feeling nervous and startled accidentally pressed harder on the accelerator and the car leapt forward.

"Aah! Brake, brake!" she screamed, her leg violently leaping about in front of him.

Then down the steep hill dead ahead, a large truck was crossing the road at traffic lights. The lights were red just like her hair!

In total confusion Dam leant forward and pressed the ejector button and in an instant shot up into the air still in a sitting position. He remembered seeing a couple of children crossing the bridge he flew over, stare open mouthed as he flew up over them, turned around still facing them and disappeared over the other side. Miraculously he landed back in his car in the driver's seat, but she had jumped across into Dam's seat and was attempting to control the car and find the brake when Dam landed in her lap facing her.

Then, smash! The car hit something. Dam didn't know what. He was jammed into her face by the air bag which had inflated and was squashing them tightly together. So tightly in fact she was biting Dam's chin!

"Argh" she said. They were stuck and couldn't move. Dam was going to ask her if she wanted to come for a Sunday drive again but couldn't move his mouth. The smell of her perfume was overpowering!

Sometime later a man opened the door of the car and found them locked together. He said,

"What do you get when you cross a blond with a red head?" The woman groaned. He then said "A very inflated bag!"

Dam was horrified as she opened her mouth and started her diesel engine which made her teeth dig in.

Dam Develops Bad Breath

Dam was no ordinary speleologist. He had a chronic fascination for holes. The larger and more mysterious the better. He would put his head into anything dark especially if it was in or near the ground. Dam loved the adventure and the feeling that perhaps he was the first person to ever venture down that dark space. He didn't mind the blackness or the close cold clamminess of a tight squeeze. He was attracted to the fear of danger, to the unknown. More than that he loved to touch the earth and to explore its internal mysteries no matter how cold and damp those mysteries might be.

Dam remembered an experience he'd had as a speleologist when he was out exploring with some friends. They were way up the side of a large mountain looking for holes and possible ways in to the centre of it. Dam had located a tunnel which he believed would lead inside the mountain to a giant cave.

"In here," he called as the other two came over. "Tight fit but I'll go in" he said. It was his idea to go caving in the first place. The small hole looked dangerous. The other two looked at each other and shook their heads.

They knew Dam liked exploring dark spaces but they certainly weren't going in there!

The hole was not much larger than Dam as he began to crawl in with the torch in his mouth. He was on his belly perhaps thirty feet in when he thought he heard a weird scratching and sliding sound quite close around a corner.

He took a large breath and the back of the torch sprang off and went down his throat with the batteries!

"Gah!" he cried out as everything went black and images of giant snakes came upon him as well as the sound of hissing! He began to wriggle backwards as fast as he could which was difficult. After scraping his nose three times and banging his head three times he began to see daylight.

"Are you alright?" exclaimed his friends. Dam rose to his feet and took the torch from his mouth and told them he'd swallowed the batteries!

"Gah" he said sticking out his tongue. He began to go a pale green colour.

"Oh no!" said his friends as they looked down his throat. "Quick, vomit!" they said as he bent over and they wacked him on the back.

"Eat this it will make you sick!" said one friend, plucking some leaves from a nearby shrub.

"Gah!" said Dam as he took a few mouthfuls and began to change from green to pink. "Gah!" he said again as his tongue and throat began to heat up with hot pins and needles from the leaves!

"Over here on this pile of leaves…. Stuff your fingers down ya throat!" they said.

"Gah! Gah!" said Dam who was beginning to feel like battery acid.

Giant snakes may have been better than this, he was thinking. He knelt down and tried to make himself sick.

"Over here!" his friends called jumping about. Soon Dam found himself being held upside down over the side of a cliff with each friend holding and shaking a leg!

It was no use the batteries and the end of the torch would not come out and Dam's tongue began to swell up and go numb from the leaves. They raced down the hill in search of water.

Over the ensuing weeks Dam had numerous stomach cramps and much wind for they had been unable to extract the batteries from Dam's diligent digestive system.

The docked-doors (doctors) tried all sorts of docked-doory things to try to get the batteries out. But Dam had an uncontrollable jaw. Anything which went down his throat a certain distance was savagely bitten off!

It was with great effort that a brand new rubber hose was retrieved after a docked-door had inserted it down Dam's throat. It took three men to pull it out and when it did come out, with a loud snap, Dam stayed in the chair and the docked-doors flew backwards across the room and crashed into trays of "sharps" as they called them! The hose had been bitten off!

Dam began to develop bad breath. He found that out when he went to the beach. There he rescued another poor swimmer from the surf, she was hardly breathing! Dam gave her mouth to mouth resuscitation and she certainly came alive quickly! Dam swears to this day that he'd saved her life!

Over the weeks his breath became worse and his teeth went green.

Not a dull green but a yellowy sort of green lighter at the tips. He started to drink lemon juice in the mornings to freshen up. When he talked to people he began to consciously breathe in for if he breathed out the people retreated some distance where Dam couldn't hear them and it was silly stepping towards them, they simply ran away!

Dam found it was difficult to breathe in as one was speaking, especially when sentences were cumbersome and long. He frequently ended up looking like a puffed up toad, his eyes bulging and his lips sucking inwards to hide his teeth. Poor Dam couldn't wait to finish digesting the batteries and hoped the lemon juice would help.

The next thing that happened to him came as the last straw! He was in town late one afternoon buying some tacks for a little window he was making when suddenly all the tacks jumped out of the box and stuck to his fingers! Dam was intrigued and waved them around! The person serving thought Dam was a magician for he thought he heard Dam say, "One, two, three!" when Dam had really said, "Well I'll be!"

Dam struggled to peel the tacks off his hands. He was very worried. The shop assistant laughed and said he was "a magnetised man" and other people came around to watch.

Dam was very embarrassed. He began to suck his mouth in and make flabby lip noises and couldn't speak. He noticed the people thought he was playing a joke so he went along with them. He found he could move his car keys around on the counter without touching them. Then he spied a light bulb, picked it up and put it in his mouth. To Dam's amazement it lit up!

The people were clapping now so Dam smiled and let out a big sigh. Instantly everybody stopped still and stood back three or more steps!

Dam paid for the tacks and left. On the way out he felt very attracted to the shovels and saws hanging in the window. He watched the saws move through the glass as though a slight breeze had disturbed them.

Dam raced home feeling positively charged. It was very hard for him to steer the car as his hands kept sticking to the steering wheel and his fingers were still covered in tacks! As he pulled himself away from his car he wondered if he was going to become any more magnetised!

"Magnetised man!" he kept saying to himself. He wondered if it was the lemon juice reacting with the batteries! He ran inside and closed the door.

He found some pliers and pulled the tacks off one by one. Then he went to the hole in the bathroom wall he had cut out for the new window. It was up high in the wall to let in more light and help dry the room. He looked down at the road and over to a nearby hill.

Dam was curious to find out more about his magnetism so he went to his electrical drawer and found another light bulb. He stuck it in his mouth and stood in front of the mirror. There was a loud pop and the bulb exploded!

Dam jumped with fright! He didn't often look in the mirror because every time he did, he received a shock. This time, to his horror, he saw that his hair was standing on end! Maybe he'd been in town with it like that! After all he was becoming forgetful as well, even though he could remember that he was forgetting things! He tried to push his hair down with his hands but it was hard and stiff!

Dam ran the bath and tested the water with his finger. Fortunately there weren't any sparks, it felt alright. He was going to get in and wash his hair. He began scratching his feet when suddenly his fingers felt tingly. He looked down and noticed sparks coming from where he was scratching.

"This will never do!" he said to himself as he tested the water with his toes.

It felt alright. When he lay down there was a small hiss so he put his hands out of the water. Slowly he put one hand in and then the other. There was a louder hiss and a cloud of small bubbles rose from his hands but nothing to worry about. Dam stretched out in his metal bath which stuck to him in places where he did not want it to stick to him!

He began to relax and ponder the day. Dam being Diligent had a particular method of washing himself which he made him very clean or so he thought.

He would roll around and around in the water like a crocodile.

Now strange things happen, let me tell you but few stranger than what then happened to Dam.

He suddenly found himself picking up speed and spinning rather fast. So fast in fact that he had to take gulps of air each time he went around! He tried to stop himself as he was becoming sick and giddy. He put his arms out like a paddle steamer but they banged into the sides of the bath. He was rapidly gathering speed! Dam was turning into an electric motor!

Now it so happened that Mrs Gravel, from next door, was coming home from a piano recital and was attracted to the sight of sparks coming from Dam Diligent's new bathroom window! She must have thought the house was on fire for she stopped the car and got out. She had her pet cat on her lap so she picked it up and was holding it when a blinding flash like a veritable lightning bolt leapt out of Dam's window accompanied by a huge explosion! Mrs Gravel got an incredible fright and threw the cat straight up in the air. Before she knew what was happening the terrified cat landed on top of her head and dug its front claws into poor Mrs Gravel's hair! Mrs Gravel screamed and banged her forehead on the tip of her car door and knocked herself clean out! And there on the road she lay with the cat curled up on her stomach underneath the stars!

Meanwhile Dam had stopped spinning after passing wind, for a terrible pain was building up inside him. He sat up in the bath which was now empty of water though he felt refreshed. As he was stepping out he slipped on something hard and round. He fell and banged his forehead on the side of the bath and knocked himself clean out! He then fell back into the bath with his feet up!

Dam woke up in the morning to the sounds of a cat at the front door.

He looked in the mirror and was surprised to see that he looked like he had big black goggles on! Both his eyes were black and their whites were red!

He smiled, he still had green teeth and his hair was still standing on end!

Off he stumbled to the door, he did not notice the batteries and the torch end in the bath!

There was Mrs Gravel's cat and down on the roadway he could see Mrs Gravel's car and there in the middle of the road forming a great bump was Mrs Gravel!

Dam immediately thought there was something wrong, perhaps she'd been run over! He quickly picked up the cat and raced down.

"Oh!" said Dam who had known Mrs Gravel for only a short while. "Mrs Gravel!" he bent down beside her. The first thing he noticed was that she had two black eyes just like his!

He patted her on the cheek and noticed she was still warm though hardly breathing. Remembering his first-aid he locked his mouth onto hers and blew as hard as he could. He watched Mrs Gravel's chest heave up and down. Fortunately she began to stir and slowly open her eyes. When she saw Dam she immediately passed out again! Dam fearing the worst felt her neck pulse.

It was slight. He quickly began to pound on her chest with his hands but soon thought it was not hard enough so he sat on her chest and began to bounce up and down!

Dam doesn't know why, but she woke up suddenly and leapt to her feet with a horrid expression on her face! She grabbed the cat, jumped in the car and without even looking at Dam, who could only smile, drove off!

Dam strolled back up to his house wondering what had frightened her and how on earth she had ended up on the road! Suddenly he realised he had forgotten to put his clothes on!

Dam Builds a Chook Pen

Dam was working on the top story of a one hundred and sixty story building. He had driven to the eightieth floor and when he got out of his car he was dizzy beyond belief and could hardly stand, let alone walk! Fortunately he spent the next half an hour going the other way and unwinding as the stairs he had to climb spiralled in the opposite direction however his head seemed to like lying on its side, that way he found he could see better. After banging his head on the first corner he changed its angle to the other side and then the other as he went around and up. He began to feel alright as he reached the top and saw the blue sky one hundred and sixty floors up.

He had been twitching wire for weeks. There was hair all over the giant contraption he was making which he called the chook pen. It was so complicated that his hair had become increasingly entangled in its thin strand which was, he believed at the time, the very thread of his existence. He said it was made of his white blood cells for he had struggled with the huge heavy bail of wire lifting it up there. How he actually managed to get it up there nobody knows for Dam was diligent and did so much that he could not remember one day from the next.

The bail of wire had so many twists and bends it was almost like a woman he mused as he stood on one end. He pushed and rolled it out after putting a weight on the end to hold it down. It was large and difficult to unwind. He had unrolled it some distance when all of a sudden it lifted the weight and rolled it inside itself as it came barrelling towards him. He held his leg up to stop it coming at him but it pushed him over and wound him up like a sausage in bread. Fortunately his other leg was trapped at an angle and prevented the bail winding further. Unfortunately he was a little stuck as the holes in the wire were exactly the same size as his nose which became jammed.

Blinking he looked threw the mesh. How would he ever get out? Squeezing two fingers through the wire he managed to push once and then twice to gain enough momentum to roll himself over. But that was no good as the wire rolled itself up again. Now he was lying on his back staring at the sky and wondering how he would ever get free! He found his clothes especially his shoes were entangled and prevented him from squeezing out.

It was some time before he was able to wriggle out one end half naked.

He had lost vast amounts of hair again and left his shirt and shoes behind and he looked like a plucked chook!

This time he made sure the end of the roll of wire was secure as he fell on his knees and began to push and unwind it again. It was springy and as long as the building was wide. The roof top was clear and flat so Dam could roll it out easily and measure it and cut it to the right size. The role became increasingly difficult to unwind and he had to use all his strength.

He had reached the end and realised he did not have another weight to hold his end down. As he was looking around for a weight the huge bail of wire lifted its weigh from the other end and came hurtling towards him. He put one leg in the air again but the bail hit him with such force that he was bowled straight over the side of the building and began to fall. The bail of wire shot over him and began to fall alongside. As they both fell at the same speed Dam realised he would have to hang onto something and he noticed that the inside of the bail was not moving at all while the outside of the wire was spinning too fast to catch. So he crawled inside the bail of wire again and lay straight and hung on! As he fell he noticed the bail was growing smaller and smaller and that the other end of the wire was still connected to the top of the building.

Then the wire stopped unravelling and he was able to see far below as he gripped the end of it. There he hung for a second, being locked in by his feet, hands and nose. But before he could think he began to spin not once but many many times as he remained in the centre of what became a huge spring.

When he finally stopped spinning and going up and down – sometime the next day – he was able to climb out exactly at the eightieth floor. Somehow, with his head to one side, he managed to get to his car and began to spiral down to the ground floor. By the time he reached the bottom floor he had already worked out how to build a flying machine, a new type of power supply, a new method of melting bees wax and how to hold your breath for an hour. He also decided to buy some eggs and make an omelette. The thought of building a chook pen made him extremely giddy.

Dam and the Catapult

Dam was in the waiting room at horse-piddle (hospital) in "casually" which was his word for Casualty. He had a piece of glass stuck in his bottom.

He was standing up against a wall as he couldn't sit down. The waiting room was full of people coughing and sneezing. There were several people behind the counter who were staring into computers and too busy to even scratch themselves. Various "docked-doors" (doctors) were coming out of rooms saying the names of people who weren't even there! Then the docked-doors disappeared and others would spring out of other rooms and say the same thing! Dam thought he may have to change his name and pretend to be someone who was not there. A few people stood up and hobbled into the little rooms and Dam could faintly hear them talking about their aches and pains.

The waiting room was hung with paintings which were all framed with expensive frames. The carpet was plush and blood red; the place exuded an ambience of wealth. All Dam wanted was an extra pair of eyes to grip the glass for he couldn't turn around and reach it properly by himself with a pair of tweezers.

He'd been waiting there for some time. He'd read all the magazines about bosoms and bottoms, love and death and war. His feet needed to move as he was naturally a very active person. He decided to ask one of the ladies behind the counter how long it would be before he would be seen.

"Which doctor?" asked the lady.

"Witch doctor!" exclaimed Dam, "I didn't know you had a witch doctor here!"

"We don't," said the lady. "Death is your doctor, I believe, do you know if it is doctor Death?"

"No, its only glass in my bottom?" said Dam and continued "I don't think it will kill me."

"No," came the reply. "Death is your doctor?"

Dam looked at her sideways, he did not understand. For a moment he thought she was putting a spell on a docked-door.

"Did he die?" asked Dam.

"No err....Mr Diligent he's alive."

"Well I hope he survives long enough to see my bottom."

"Doctor Mybotum is not in today."

"But how can I see a dead witch doctor?" asked Dam.

"Just task a seat," said the lady.

"No thank you, I have plenty already," he said.

Just then there was a loud crash as one of the paintings fell off the wall and smashed on the floor. It was a photograph of a white person shaking the hand of a small black person. The glass in the frame broke and went all over the floor.

Some children were running around shouting and screaming in the corridor but they soon stopped and looked at the glass.

"Stand back!" said Dam, who at the time was working at a picture framing business where he'd had his accident with the glass. "Glass is dangerous," he said.

Dam knew all about picture framing. He'd been working in the business for exactly half a day and he'd already managed to smash every piece of glass he touched. Until one particularly nasty piece speared him in the bottom.

He told his boss that he didn't think he was cut out for the job but his boss said you'll be alright after a day or two.

Dam bent down to pick up the glass on the floor and the spear of glass in his bottom dug in deeper.

"I'll fix this for you," he said. "My picture framing business will fix it."

To cut a long story short, Dam took the measurements of the frame, had the glass removed and with a large bandage on his bottom went back to work.

He began to cut the glass and this time did it correctly without cracking it.

He put it in his car and took it back to the waiting room. However on the way there it fell over in the car and broke.

Damn said Dam as he went back to the glass factory and cut another piece. But as he was carrying it up the stairs to the waiting room he dropt it and it smashed. He went back to the factory and cut another piece. This time he actually managed to put it in the frame but as he was hanging it up on the wall it fell from his hands and the glass smashed! He sped back to the factory and cut another piece.

"This is ridiculous" he said to himself, there must be a better way to make money. He took the glass to the waiting room again. The same people were still waiting there. The children stood back. He placed it in the frame and hung it on the wall very carefully. And this time it worked. He backed away carefully and tip-toed down the stairs to his car.

When he slammed the door of his car the picture fell off the wall and smashed again but Dam did not know.

He went back to his work and kept breaking glass. At the end of the day he'd filled a large barrel with broken glass. His boss said,

"Well done Mr Diligent, now please don't come back tomorrow!"

Poor Dam went home very depressed. He had a large bandage on his bottom and a heavy feeling was within him.

"How shall I make money?" he asked himself.

He stayed at home for a few days until his bottom healed. He ate rice and beans and emptied his money box.

Close to where Dam lived was a famous surfing beach which had a beautiful wave. The swells peeled off a rocky point and formed a very good wave for surfing. When the swell was large it was very hard for surfers to paddle out. Then one day he designed a huge catapult for throwing people into the sea. Strange as it sounds that is exactly what it was. So Dam decided to build his catapult way out on the headland and throw surfers out into the water.

He had no money. He ate wild vegetables which he found growing on the headland. He drank spring water which flowed from the hill and at night he watched the dancing stars and listened to the roaring surf as he slept sometimes in a small cave.

He began to make rope from the leaves of the pandanus trees which grew on the headland and he fashioned the long-throw arm from a large piece of drift wood. After sometime his catapult was ready and he winched the powerful throw-arm back under great strain and put a large rock in it which he reckoned was the same weight as a man.

He pulled the trigger rope and with an almighty "whoomp" the stone flew up in the air and far out to sea where it made a white splash like the spout of a whale.

"I will need a volunteer astronaut." Dam said to himself and wondered if anybody would be brave enough to try.

He did not have to wait long as the sea began to break wildly in the night and in the morning many people with surfboards stood on the rocks in front of the catapult. Dam sat beside it looking very thin.

"Great waves!" he said to a young boy.

"Yeah," replied the boy.

"Difficult paddle." Dam said.

"Yeah," said the boy.

"I've got a catapult to fling you out beyond the break if you want."

"Yeah!" said the boy a little louder.

Dam sat him in the firing position and was ready to let the trigger go.

"Whoomp!"

"Yeeaahh!" screamed the boy as he was hurled high into the air way out past the breaking waves where he crashed into the water and made a splash the size of a breaching whale!

Other surfers saw him flying overhead.

"Oh wow!" they all said, "Can we have a go!?"

"Yes of course," said Dam. "Cost you fifty cents."

Whoomp, whoomp, whoomp, Dam was kept busy all day.

He soon had a stack of coins piling up in his cave and over the next four weeks the surf was large every day. Dam's pile of money grew and grew.

Several months passed and Dam made many friends. He was becoming richer and richer.

"Sure beats cutting glass!" he said to himself. He still lived off wild plants, ate shellfish and drank spring water though.

Until one day he decided to go to the bank and deposit all his money.

He spent the whole day carrying bags of it up to his car. The bank people spent hours and hours counting it. Dam found himself waiting again. He hated waiting! After they'd finished counting Dam went out and bought himself a meal and after that he had a milk shake. He was so full he could barely move and he had a terrible pain in his tummy. He drove back to his cave on the headland and drunk lots of spring water.

Over the next few years Dam made lots of money. His cave was full of it. Some nights it gleamed in the moonlight.

He looked at his great pile of coins and said that it was quite useless just lying there. He kept taking it to the bank and had to wait hours for it to be counted. Dam would spend the time talking to the bank teller. Then one day he found out the fellow's name, it was Death. Dam looked pale as he watched his nimble fingers flick through the coins like fragments of splintered glass.

Back on the headland he loved to watch the moon rise over the ever changing sea and listen to the sound of the singing waves on the rocks.

He needed nothing more. The food he ate kept him alive and the people he met made him laugh. Every now and then he had to visit the bank to get rid of his money. One day he looked at the amount he had and saw that he had enough to buy a property with a creek and lots of trees. This he did but it was a long time before he left his whispering cave and began to build a house in the silent countryside.

Dam Builds With Clay

One day Dam had a memorable experience with herbicide on his property.

He had just finished stirring a large drum of it and was using the drum to stand on to pick a bunch of bananas when the lid caved in and he fell into the drum! That day he had turned pink then purple then white and his nose turned yellow like a banana, all in the one day!

After that he decided to stop using chemicals and decided to begin to recycle his rubbish. He also threw away his electric fridge to save energy and bought a gas one but it kept going out and he had to crawl on the floor with a match to light it all the time. He was growing tired of that.

He also decided to use mud bricks to build with and to tie his garbage up in small bags and use them as waterproofing under the foundations of the new room he was building. He was going to use recycled timber from now on and recycle his garbage and use mud and clay to build the room with because it was free of poisonous chemicals.

The roof was going to be garbage and then earth on top of that. Dam was enthusiastic about his idea and began to collect his garbage rather than take it to the tip. He started to make his clay bricks by hand. After sometime he had a huge stack of rubbish and a huge stack of bricks.

He set to work. First he dug a hole the size of the floor area, this he filled with his bags of garbage twenty centimetres thick. Then he covered that with a copper pipe for he was going to heat the floor with solar hot water.

Dam covered the floor with clay and wood ash thirty centimetres thick.

It took ages for the floor to dry, it was sticky but Dam didn't mind he just wore his gum boots. Soon the mud brick walls were up and then the roof. He put a skylight in the roof for extra light and on hot days he could open it for air.

The ceiling of the roof he made with more garbage bags, wood and then mud and then soil. He hand made all the windows and doors which took ages as Dam was diligent and meticulous in his work.

The room was finished and began to dry out. It had cost him very little and was not poisonous. He planted grass on the roof and kept it short with a pair of shears as his lawn-mower polluted the air. He wound some black water-pipe around the roof so it would heat up from the sun and warm the floor below by circulating the water.

It was summer though and the room seemed to stay a nice cool temperature. After a few hot days Dam decided to move the fridge inside the room where the wind would not blow the flame out and he hoped it would stay a little cooler.

Dam redesigned his toilet so the sediment would flow down the hill and feed his orchard which was some distance from the house. He began to notice however that it was rather smelly and one hot day when the smell was almost unbearable on the hot wind, he went into his cool room.

He remembers the day well, for he noticed the fridge had gone out in the breeze and the whole place seemed to smell of gas. As he bent down to strike a match there was a terrific explosion. He recalled being blasted up into the air and out through the skylight! Daylight appeared around the edges of the ceiling. There was a great rushing noise and he seemed to go up and up forever.

Dam opened his eyes for he could still smell something. He was wet all over and soon realised he'd landed in part of his new toilet. The fridge was lying beside him as well as large bits of his room. He wasn't cold but there seemed to be snow everywhere! He was lucky to be alive he thought.

As he walked back to the house he noticed that all the windows had been blown out. And as he looked closer he saw that it wasn't snow which lay about but tiny little pieces of plastic garbage!

Dam and the Bees

Dam looked at his hands, they were getting old. The creases and the scars were crusting over like Gondwana land masses on earth and when he clenched his fist the continents moved but then he couldn't get his hands to open again! He had found that putting them in ice eased the pain. It was sometime before he could hold a spoon and feed his cracked dry lips which once apart were difficult to close.

"Arthritis!" he said to himself. His scrawny arm resembled a ragged mainsail hanging off the boom, the flesh hung down in slithers like honey and he imagined his rude finger might melt if he stirred his cup of tea with it. He put his hands away where he couldn't see them, as far away as he could. The wind rustled in the trees outside so Dam rose with difficulty to see what they were waving at.

A warm scented breeze wafted about him and he saw that the tree in his front yard was in flower. The hum of bees buzzed in his ears and as he watched he remembered that the tree was hollow. Dam had found a hole down near the ground a few days before and wondered if anything lived in there. The tree had another hole in the top in between two branches. Now coming and going from the top hole was a steady stream of bees.

Dam being diligent was familiar with bee hives. He'd helped his brother Justin raid a bee hive once. Dam was in charge of the long-nosed pliers which he planned to use justin case any bees entered under Justin's veil. Fortunately no bees did as Dam had lost the pliers well before they had started and Justin was not prepared to raid the hive without them! One

33

couldn't be too sure without pliers he said and if the bees stung you on the inside under the veil, well you had to get out to the outside as quickly as possible and that was damn hard to do and was usually a two person job as all the holes were taped up, justin case. Justin and Dam took hours to dress. Dam was done-up with tape, overalls, boots, glasses, goggles, veil, and gloves which were too big to operate pliers with anyway! And if a bee crawled under the veil it was impossible to get it off in time and all you could do was run for it and that was the silliest thing you could do as the bee could see you were scarred and would sting you if you didn't have pliers!

Dam flexed his hands and decided to raid the tree. It took him an hour to get ready and find his plastic overalls and the smoker, matches, bucket for honey, veil, gloves, boots, hat, pliers, matches, wood, paper and leaves.

He also brought along a fly swat, a hammer and a rolled up newspaper and just in case, some extra tape and a pair of scissors.

He spent a long while dressing in front of the mirror. Then with all his equipment he walked out the door. Dam was a warrior dressed in white even though he could hardly move. He was ready for the worst scenario and this time he had the pliers!

It was a little difficult bending down to look in the hole as he was taped up around the eyes and his goggles banged on the tree. The bottom of the veil creased slightly and revealed a little hole and Dam hoped no bees were intelligent enough to find it. Justin case he straightened up to check and luckily the hole disappeared.

Listening carefully he could hear the bees humming in the hollow of the giant tree like a didgeridoo or a voice from times past before the age of men when bees were fashioning their poison and sharpening their spears.

To raid a bee hive one needs a smoker. This is a little device which puffs smoke into the hive. The smoke makes the bees eat honey as they think a fire is coming and once they are full of honey they are less likely to sting you.

Dam made ready to light the smoker. He fumbled for the matches which were in his pocket. But he couldn't open the box with his big gloves on, let alone strike a match! So he had to take his gloves off. He stuffed paper and leaves into the smoker. He struck a match and set the smoker alight. There was a sudden roar of flame and the smoker went out! He stuffed more paper and leaves in as well as some sticks. This time it seemed to stay alight so he put his gloves back on and taped up his sleeves. By the time his gloves were on, the smoker was out. He took his gloves off and began to think. The wind rustled in the leaves above him and the dull roar of bees sounded like his brain thinking.

Dam stood up and walked towards his garden hose. He took it off the tap and began to push it up inside the tree. He theorised that if he twisted the hose around and around it would knock the honeycomb off the walls then he would be able to collect the honey at ground level. Maybe the honey would just pour down the hose and into his bucket!

Up and up the hose went and the roar of the bees became louder. Suddenly a bee flew out of the hole in front of him and went straight for him, hit the veil and bounced off. Dam stopped twisting the hose as the smoker was out and began to fumble with the match box which sprung open flinging matches everywhere. Dam being diligent took his gloves off again and picked up every one, then relit the smoker. This time he piled leaves, twigs and sticks and branches in. He pointed it in the hole and huffed and puffed till the tree was full of smoke and clouds of it began to billow out from the top of the trunk.

The bees went into a feeding frenzy with the roaring voice of a million beating wings. The whole tree trunk began to roar and vibrate like a large didgeridoo, it sounded like it would explode! Dam began twisting the hose more and more forcefully. Bees appeared at the hole, crawling around on the ground then a large chunk of honeycomb fell and slid down the hose! He put it in his bucket. Soon another piece fell down, then another and another.

Dam stood back amazed as honey began to flow out of the tree. Soon his bucket began to fill to overflowing! But that wasn't all, gradually the sleeve of a shirt appeared! It was Dam's shirt, his floral one! He hadn't seen it since he wore it to his neighbour's birthday party! That was when they'd found him in the tree the next day. Dam pulled on the sleeve and it slewed down with a large glob of honey.

He knelt down and scooped the honey up with his gloved hands. A few bees flew down and disappeared past his face and he waved them away as they flew past. Unfortunately his hand caught his veil slightly and stuck there. He pulled it away from the veil with his other hand and soon there was honey all over his veil! His smoker had gone out again and he tried to stand up but couldn't; he was stuck to the ground! He pushed himself up and leaves stuck to his hands!

A few bees came about him so he grabbed the fly-swat and thrashed the air violently. Another bee came, then another and another. Dam being diligent swatted them out of the air.

The bees were angry, their hum was growing louder, a few more had descended to his level and one was interested in the honey on the veil.

The smoker had gone out so Dam began to take off his gloves again in order to strike a match. Honey was everywhere, he was tramping around in it and bees were coming in numbers to take their honey back. Determined to press on, Dam stuffed the smoker full of newspaper and leaves, occasionally stopping to lash out with the fly-swat.

Miraculously he lit the smoker as it was still warm, then he shrieked with fright as something had stung him on the leg! No he was burning! The smoker had melted his plastic overalls and left a large hole in his pants! He watched in horror as the round piece of plastic turned black as it melted on the smoker and dripped on the ground where it mingled with the honey.

Bees were about and Dam struck out with the smoker. It went out again so he knelt down in the pool of honey and not thinking rested the smoker on the other leg and tried to light it. He took the gloves off again and fumbled with the sticky matches. The smoker burst into flames and Dam luxuriated in clouds of smoke. Suddenly he shot in the air something had stung him on the other leg! No the hot smoker had burnt another hole in his plastic overalls! He held the smoker up and watched the plastic drip into the pool of honey on the ground. He looked at the two large holes in his pants and saw that his skin was badly burnt. His legs were still warm. At least he had honey to put on the burns he thought.

Dam huffed and puffed the smoker so much that from a distance he looked like he was on fire! But then the smoker went out! The matches lay on the ground in honey along with his gloves. His boots were stuck, he lifted them slowly and his foot came out of one boot! He was just about to put it back in when a bee climbed under the veil, walked up his neck and balanced on his nose in front of his goggles! Dam went cross-eyed as he watched it trying to free its own legs from honey.

He tried to blow it off, huffing and puffing but it remained on his nose. With one leg in the air he searched the ground for the pliers. He couldn't see them anywhere. Cross-eyed he could see the bee's sting aiming at his nose! Out of shear fear he wacked himself on the nose and unfortunately the sting was forced deep into the tip of his nose! The squashed bee hung there joined to his nose by the sting which began to wobble as it went in deeper.

Dam yelled with pain. All of a sudden something tickled his leg then another and another. The bees had found the holes in his pants and were climbing up his legs towards a delicate place! Dam became scarred and banged his pants furiously. Now he was being stung inside his pants! Poor Dam let out a loud wail and began to hobble, hop and run over to the garden hose. It had gone! Some person had taken the hose!

Dam's legs seemed on fire, he was banging his bottom and still being stung as he launched himself inside the house followed by a cloud of bees and raced up the stairs into the shower. He stood under the water fully dressed in his bee outfit! With his hat, veil and goggles still on, with one boot on and began squashing all the bees he could with his bare hands. Then he filled the bath with cold water and climbed in with his clothes still on and under his veil he crossed his eyes and noticed the sting still hanging from his nose.

Dam struggled to remove his clothes in the bath. He took the veil off and removed the sting from his nose which became so large he couldn't breathe through it! He took his overalls off and a scum of bees floated to the surface. His legs which felt like red hot lumps of jelly, had bee stings all over them. Staring at the ceiling beyond his nose, his heart rate began to increase. He sunk low in the water and was just about to pass out when he smelt smoke. He lifted an eye lid and tried to move but he was stuck. Smoke was coming in the door and he could hear the sound of crackling flames! He launched himself from the bath and ran to the top of the stairs.

Dam's house was on fire! Being diligent and naked he ran back to the bath and looked around for the bucket but some person had taken the bucket!

He quickly grabbed his plastic overalls and tied knots in the legs to put water in. Then scooped out his hat and veil and looked around for the bucket again.

He grabbed his hat and began to scoop water out of the bath furiously and throw it down the stairs. Dam was lucky, he managed to put the fire out! He hobbled down the stairs and found the smoker at the bottom!

Dam looked in the mirror at his nose, it was huge and swollen. His breathing sounded like the smoker. He made himself some lemon tea and ate all his oranges to prevent a histamine reaction and hoped that his swelling would go down. He dragged his one-boot-leg over to the sofa and sat down.

Dam dreamed he was a bee. A loud humming sound filled his ears. He flew around and around. The countryside looked very green. He came to a tree covered in blossom, there was a hole in the tree and Dam, as a bee, was attracted to the hole. But a great white bear with a funny hat was banging on the trunk of the tree which was annoying. He flew at the bear and stung him on the nose!

Dam woke up he was in horse-piddle (hospital). The fan on the ceiling was turning round and round. Orange and black stripped nurses with wings on were leaning over him. Their eyes were unbelievably huge. One of them leaned over him with a large needle the size of a bee sting and said "Buzz!"

Dam struggled but his muscles felt like runny honey. He reached up and grasped the needle as best he could and used it like a fly-swat. He wacked the air with it and the nurses went away. Still clutching the great needle he ran out of the horse-piddle all the way home. As he was running he noticed his feet were barely touching the ground and he was dressed in white. The needle was still clasped tightly in his hand.

Dam woke up. He was still in the bath. His nose was making loud hissing noises as he exhaled and ringlets of small waves expanded from his chin.

He was not in any pain. Indeed he felt fantastic. He leapt out of the bath splashing water everywhere. He got back in the bath and got out again because he could not believe that he had no pain and he liked to splash water everywhere! He reached for the towel but his hand was closed tightly. Miraculously it opened without him having to use the other hand to help!

He nimbly stretched his legs, no pain. He looked at his overalls in the bath, his hat, veil and boot amongst the dozens of floating bees. He dressed and went downstairs. He hadn't felt this well in years! He looked outside and a slight breeze waved in the trees.

The sun was shining and the garden looked dry. He went over to the tap to water the garden and found that the hose had gone! Then he remembered the bee tree so he cautiously went over to have a look. There on the ground was a huge mound of bees. They were claiming their honey back! And somebody had jammed half his hose up inside the tree!

"Oh well!" sighed Dam, feeling his nose. As he turned to go back inside a bee flew past his ear - so he hastened his pace. He went into the kitchen thinking of toast and honey but the honey pot was empty and there on the table he found the pliers! He picked them up and put them in his pocket Justin case. He felt his burnt legs and wished he had some honey to put on the burns. He looked outside at the honey tree and the hordes of bees on the ground and in the air. He turned the radio on and the first thing he heard was,

"Some arthritis sufferers find their aches and pains disappear after a bee sting." Dam looked out the window again. The great mound of bees looked like an animal at the foot of the tree, menacing and moving. Dam opened and closed his hands and felt the pliers. He licked his lips as the taste of honey buzzed across his mind.

"I think I'll raid the bees" he said out loud.

Dam and the Flea

Something jumped out of Dam's beard. He looked, there was a flea in his tea! It seemed to be lying on its back paddling around! Dam fetched the spoon and tried to rescue the poor thing! But it would not be rescued and kept diving under and surfacing in other places, then it began to paddle around lying on its back again! Dam watched for a while as it did breast stroke and duck dived like a dolphin. Dam put the spoon in gently and the flea came over to it and climbed up out of the tea. Dam lifted it out and put it in a little puddle of tea on the table.

The flea stood up, shook itself then marched over to a grain of rice which was left on the table and lifted it up and down. Dam looked in amazement as this rather large flea began to hold the grain of rice on its end and throw it in the air and catch it by the other end. But that was not all, the flea soon spied another grain of rice and it wasn't long before it was juggling both rice grains and catching them by their ends!

Dam tore around the house to look for his camera. He did not believe what he was seeing and needed to photograph it to prove it. He looked under the stairs but hit his head on a stair, he looked inside a drawer but got his finger stuck in the drawer. Then he remembered and went to the oven put his hand in and pulled out the camera. He had put it in there a week earlier as he'd heard about a woman who had cooked her arm after she had left it in the oven! He put the camera in there to remind himself not to leave his arm in the oven. Dam was used to himself doing things sometimes which he knew he shouldn't do so he had to watch himself so he did not do what he did not mean to do...or did.

Racing back to the flea he dropped the camera on the floor and trod on it.

The camera was alright but his foot was badly twisted and he jumped about on one leg for a while. He surveyed the table for his little acrobat. He looked in the cracks and bent low to scan the surface with his moon-like eyes.

Unknown to Dam the flea had been frightened when it saw Dam hit his head on the stairs and jam his finger in the drawer. And when he dropped the camera and began to leap around the room the flea had become even more frightened and leapt off the table onto the floor where it hid under one of the table legs.

There it stayed with a tummy full of rice and tea peering out watching Dam.

Dam looked everywhere and photographed his table anyway, sometimes pictures reveal things we cannot see he said.

Next morning Dam had two grains of rice waiting for the giant flea to come. He kept scratching his beard and looking in his tea. He made two cups just in case.

It took Dam sometime to get over the acrobatic flea. He told the lady in the bread shop that he would bring a photograph of it one day.

That is why when one has tea at Dam's place, many years later, there is still a camera and two grains of rice on the table waiting for a little acrobatic flea to fall from Dam's beard.

Dam and the Spider

One morning Dam was listening to the radio when a program came on about spiders and how poisonous they were. The program talked about what to do if one is bitten by a certain black spider. Some people had been made seriously ill by this spider and some had even died.

The next day Dam was in his garden when he stepped back and felt something spike him on the leg. He leapt up in the air with a great cry thinking a spider had bitten him. He raced inside and quickly took off his boot and washed the small wound.

As the wound began to sting he quickly ran to his car with one boot on but had to hop back inside as he'd forgotten his car keys. As he tore along the highway on his way to horse-piddle (hospital) he came upon a red traffic light. While he stopped he considered that he should have tied something around his leg to slow the poison down. He took off his shirt and tore a sleeve off it and wrapped the sleeve around his leg and tied it as tightly as he could. The light had gone green long ago and cars were beeping their horns behind him. The bite began to sting and ache. Dam's heart began to pound!

At the horse-piddle he nearly drove up the steps at Casually (Casualty).

He leapt out of his car and grabbed his sleeveless shirt and hopped up the stairs half naked as quickly as he could with one boot on. He slumped on the desk, the poison was taking effect!

"Please," he moaned "spider bite!" He slumped to the floor and began frothing at the mouth. The secretary leaned over the counter and asked him if he was alright. Dam moaned, his leg developed an uncontrollable twitch.

Soon people in white coats came leisurely along the corridor and put him on a stretcher. They seemed so slow. Dam closed his eyes and felt his heart beat.

It felt like an egg in an egg beater.

He was taken into Emergency and various wires were stuck onto him so that he could see himself on screens bleeping on and off.

"Am I alright, am I going to die?" he asked.

"We can't tell yet" said the nurse and added, "if you die we'll tell you.

What sort of spider was it?"

"A big one," said Dam whose eyes were beginning to roll around in his head. The spider bite was stinging and throbbing, the pain was more than he could stand so he began to moan and groan again.

Several hours passed and gradually the pain subsided. Dam reckoned he was going to survive. They came and took blood from him but found it very difficult as Dam's muscles were so tense the needles kept bending.

"Mr Diligent you're fine," they told him. "You've been cut by a sharp object that's all."

"Oh!" said Dam somewhat relieved. His bed was warm and he liked watching the beeps on the screen.

"We'll give you a tetanus injection, now roll over."

"Roll over!" said Dam, who had never had a tetanus injection before.

"Yes" said the nurse, "we have to administer it in your bottom."

"Oh," said Dam squinting a little.

Unfortunately the nurse found it very difficult to get the needle to go in. Three needles bent and one broke off. Dam couldn't feel a thing and after some time wondering what was going on he rolled over just in time to see an ugly black spider holding the huge needle way above her head about to plunge it into his bottom like a sting.

"Argh" said Dam as his leg suddenly left the bed and met with the nurse's arm as the needle was coming down. The needle missed Dam altogether and stuck in the nurses breast where it hung next to her name tag.

"Oh, I'm so sorry" he said.

Dam picked his one boot up, found his shirt without the sleeve and drove home with a bandage on his small wound. His bottom felt a little sore.

"Typical" he said, "I go to horse-piddle with a sore leg and come out with a sore bottom!"

Next day Dam was out digging in his garden again when a small spider ran over his hand. He shrieked, threw the shovel in the air and ran inside. Now he was having visions of huge spiders climbing in through the windows. Dam went to the window and looked outside. Sure enough there was a huge black spider coming down the path towards him. He rubbed his eyes in disbelief and looked again. No it wasn't a spider it was only the postman.

Dam Starts a Clothes Shop

Dam was a keen needle-worker. He'd made quite a name for his way-out fashion designs. His most notable to date was an evening dress covered in fiberglass which made the wearer dance uncontrollably.

Other notable designs he had made included see through windows which revealed painted body parts surrounded by flashing lights. Dam had impeccable taste when it came to design. A recent success was an the outfit which made the wearer look like a plastic wrapped box of meat from the supermarket. The red tee-shirt read, "Hold me close, I'll be yours tonight" then the words "Use By" written on the back.

Dam liked hiding batteries in clothing, they gave that illuminating flash when least expected. One patron fell in the sea off a ship at night and was only found because she was flashing! Dam put lights under hats and in out of the way places. He made lace trimmings with minute coloured light bulbs which were powered by tiny generators hidden in the shoes so that with each step a surge of light would envelop an arm or leg like a swarm of fire flies!

Dam had small generators in hidden pockets all over the place. One long pair of boots had magnets around both knees. This design needed fine tuning after one wearer walked quickly which caused the voltage surge which made her knees lock together!

These unique clothes had to be very safe and the wearer had to be fully insured against fire and electric shock. This became necessary after a full length body stocking short-circuited and began to melt onto its wearer. The large band around the neck suddenly began to constrict.

Dam had other close calls too. Especially when a stroboscopic hair-piece caught fire and made the wearer throw champagne all over her head to put out the blaze. The unfortunate wearer spent a long time after that in horse-piddle (hospital) with her head in a plastic bag!

"Dam Diligent Fashions" generated quite a name for himself and one had to be extremely brave to even go into his shop at times.

His luck turned or so he thought it did, when a large swim-ware company rang and asked if he could design some new season swim ware.

Dam immediately set about designing a very evocative piece for men.

It consisted of a single fig leaf and a matching nautical cap. The cap was electronically lit for easy detection in the surf.

Both items were a fantastic success especially since his male model was sick on the preview evening and Dam had to walk the cat-walk and display it himself.

The first thing that went wrong was that he had an adverse reaction to the fig leaf. His skin suddenly started to itch and sting. When he was on the catwalk he found he could barely control himself and by the time he'd reached the end of it he was in a very sorry state! He kept crossing and uncrossing his knees! Apart from that, all the ladies in the audience began to shriek with laughter. And Dam's embarrassment was not in the least bit relieved when he covered himself with the cap. Quite the reverse! There was a sudden flash of light and puff of smoke and Dam hobbled off stage, his legs wide apart - daring not to look!

Those few moments certainly ended his own modelling career and he was put out of action for quite some time!

Dam Has a Visitor

One day Dam was full of energy and sprang out of bed as though he'd been bitten by something. The day was miserable and overcast. Soon he was picking up clothes with one hand while in the other he held his breakfast of cold green beans and mustard. Presently there was a tap on the front door. Dam had actually fixed a real tap there the day before as a door-knocker but this was a little tap; light at first then louder and faster. He stood up and went and opened the door.

There before him was a huge spider, bigger than a car, black and hairy! Almost at once a clawed arm landed on his shoulder, he fended it off with a quick jab. Then another arm came upon him suddenly from the side! Again he fended it off diligently. Dam realised he was being attacked by the spider its great black bulk was nearly upon him and he could feel other arms about him and the fangs…

Quick as a flash he thrust his mustard and beans in the spider's face. He heard a kind of grunting and gurgling sound and he was released for a split second.

Dam began to fear for his life as he thought mustard and beans may have a beneficial effect on giant spiders. He sprang up onto the ceiling and held on by his hands to a rafter then swung backwards and fell face down onto the back of the spider. The spider made a strange gurgling sound like it was sucking its lips then reared up on its back legs and fell over backwards, dead, with Dam underneath! He was temporarily squashed before he managed to wriggle out.

Something was stinging the front of him and when he looked he found he had lots of spider's hairs sticking out of his chest like straws. He stood there pulling them out and throwing them on the floor.

Suddenly the spider shot into the air and landed on its feet. By the time it had landed Dam was inside his house locking the door with the tap on it. The spider did not use the tap and started banging on the door. Dam ran around the house looking for weapons to use to defend himself. He found an old Viking helmet and a twelfth century axe which his great, great, great, great, great, great, great, great, great, great, great, great grandfather had used for the invasion of England. He found some big boots and a pair of dark glasses. He found some strong pants and a big coat and a pair of gloves. If the spider was going to bite him he'd need good strong clothing on!

He could hear the spider walking around the house. He quickly ran to the kitchen and ate half a jar of mustard thinking it may be useful at close range. Then he climbed up on the bench and hid in a kitchen cupboard. He left the cupboard door open a little because one boot and the axe didn't fit inside.

Dam could hear the spider on the veranda. Now he could see it as it moved past the kitchen window. It turned and faced the glass. Was it going to break the glass and come inside? Dam gripped the handle of his axe.

The spider's maw decorated the window its great fangs trying to pierce the glass. The hairy convoluted mouth occasionally showing a deep red vortex, reminded Dam of a live volcano. The fangs looked like a bent fork-lift.

He shut his eyes. Then loud banging, then quiet – now the spider was on the roof! He could hear its many legs walking up the ridge. Dam was in a top cupboard and he could feel the whole building shake as though it was an earthquake.

Dam flung open the cupboard door and was thrown onto the kitchen floor. Fortunately he landed on his head and the helmet saved him. Though it did become jammed but not so much that he could not see. He had to lift his head well back to see where or which way to go.

He staggered to the window. The shaking reached a crescendo then all was quiet.

Had the spider jumped off? Dam looked out and yes, he could see it some distance off loping along near his tractor. It looked like a large combine harvester. Dam watched it kick up dust as it turned and went down the road.

He strained his back to an upright position and gripped the horns of his helmet. He sat on the floor gripping them as he tried to get his head unstuck. Whoever wore the helmet before must have had a small head! He couldn't loosen it. After sometime he decided it was safe to go outside.

Still dressed in battle gear he stepped out onto the veranda looking both ways, up and down. It was then that he realised why it had been such an overcast day for the whole house was covered in cobweb! The sun above had been blocked out! Dam walked to the edge of the veranda and prodded the web with his axe. The whole net wobbled and moved.

Would the spider come back? Was he trapped in his own house? Was he about to become beans and mustard, a spider's lunch? He ran back inside but was violently pulled backwards by something. When he turned around he realised the horns of the helmet were stuck in the cobweb! Dam gripped them again but it was no good. He was trapped like a fly and maybe the spider would return very soon!

Dam Learns to Meditate

The bells were ringing as Dam walked up the stairs. The incense was pungent and clouds of it wafted around the large oak doors like spirits of the dead enticing people into the great hall of truth where their mendacious meanderings would be exorcised from them like rotten teeth and strewn before the altar of God to be morphed into the pious purity of gold.

The sonorous sound of the bells reverberated in the hollowness of his chest and the ringing harmonics strung chords between his heart strings and his wobbling ear lobes as the animal hairs bristled down his back and out along his arms to his electric eel fingertips.

Dam entered the church. He sat down on the highly polished pew and wiped a little dribble from his chin. A picture of Mother Mary looked graciously down at him. Churches made him feel sleepy. His breathing became rhythmic, his tongue slightly out, the faulty lights were flickering.

Bang! He hit his head on the pew in front of him; wobbly and sleepy. Bang he did it again! This time he fell in between the seats and lay on the floor, the incense wafting over him like the pulsing of the bells. There he lay gently breathing. He felt warm and quiet, his little bag of shopping no longer straining his arms. Sometime later he heard voices and he woke up.

He was cold. The ceiling was white and lit by harsh strips of neon light.

The smell of the place assailed him. He sat up. Where was he? In horse-piddle (hospital)? An elderly gent lay on another bed next to him.

"My," thought Dam "he does look sick!" And another person on the other side! But he looked dead! Dam jumped off the bed and was walking over to a door when it opened and a man wearing spectacles and a white coat entered.

"Arggh!" cried the man, who went pale and dropped his book. "You're meant to be dead!"

"Dead!" said Dam. "Is this a Morgue?"

"Sure is," said the man who looked pale and flabby like rice pudding gone wrong.

"Well I'm as alive as you!" Dam said remembering he was in Church the last he could recall. And was this the heaven he'd come to see finally? Some church if it had that effect on people. No, this was hell, it smelt like his great aunt!

Sometime later Dam found himself in a bus without his little bag of shopping. He just stared out the window at the people in the street. They were all like him or would be one day. And when they were all old they would end up in the morgue too. Dam wondered how long it would be before he ended up back there fully out to it, perhaps entering the doors of heaven or just standing outside the doors of hell, sniffing. He began to wonder what it was that made people age so quickly. Was it what they ate or what they did? For instance whether they were happy or sad. Just then the bus passed a sign which read, "Live longer, relieve stress and meditate."

Dam made a mental note of the contact number, reiterating it many times to himself as he didn't have a pen to write it down. When he reached home he rang the number but it was the wrong one. He wondered if relieving stress had anything to do with remembering things. Since he had reached one hundred and twenty five years of age his memory had become less accurate.

The sign read, "Meditate for a long life." Dam stood outside the room where one went to learn how to meditate. He'd booked himself in for classes! This day he was unusually dressed for Dam, in a coat and new shoes.

He opened the door. The smell of incense assailed him. His eyes went red and he began to cough uncontrollably. A lady behind a desk offered him some water. She spoke so well and was beautiful. He took the water and gulped it down the wrong way. He held his breath momentarily before blasting it back out all over the poor woman and the desk.

"Aargh!" he said still coughing and spluttering.

"Oh, (hick)... I am (hick) so (hick) sorry, argh!" he said trying to control the hiccups. "Your appointment is not till next week," the lady said.

Dam stood in front of the door a week later he had his gas mask on and he'd brought a drink container. "Your appointment is tomorrow" Mr Diligent said the same lady.

Dam quickly got out of the room. He hadn't cleaned the gas mask since WW1 and he'd swallowed a lot of dust the wrong way. Worse than that a spider has run across the glass inside just as he was opening the door. Outside the room he coughed and coughed and his hiccups returned. He drank some water upside down backwards by suspending himself from the handrail by his knees but he still hiccupped all the way down the stairs and home.

Next day Dam stood at the door again. He'd cleaned the gas mask and had his drink bottle under his arm. Meanwhile he'd read up on how to stop hiccups and he'd brought along an electric light cord with exposed wires at one end.

He learned that hiccups were caused by stress and were an electrical phenomena involving the nervous system. Dam thought he could plug the lead in, hold the end of it and shock the hiccups away.

He entered the room. The woman behind the desk rolled her eyeballs to the ceiling, she was good at that. This time Dam was on time. The lady spoke to somebody who said they would be out shortly. Dam stood there with the electric light lead in one hand and bottle of water in the other, his clean gas mask on and a little bag of shopping strapped to his back. Through the mask Dam eyed a power point just in case. He stood in front of the desk waiting.

Quite a few moments passed and the secretary opened a drawer and pulled out a packet of cigarettes.

"Oh no!" thought Dam who was allergic to tobacco smoke. He stood there talking and shaking his head, pointing at the already lit cigarette. It was no good, she didn't understand. He took the mask off just as the side door opened and the weirdest looking person came out of a black room. He had long hair and a long grey beard. He stepped over to Dam and held out his hand. "Please don't do that" said Dam as he was assailed by tobacco smoke and incense. He put the mask back on and tried to supress a cough. His eyes began to bulge so fearing the worst he jammed the electric lead into the power socket and turned it on.

He then shook the man's hand, coughing. The gas mask flew a foot out from his face and sprang back.

Well you should have seen the long haired man's reaction! His hair stood straight up from his head and emitted blue sparks! He seemed to leap about the room uncontrollably for ages screaming, still holding Dams hand. Dam saw the man's hair begin to smoke and then suddenly explode in flames. Dam tipped his water bottle all over him and he shot in the air again! Steam was springing forth like plumes of incense. The man let out an incredible cry of agony and disappeared back into his black room!

No hiccups! Dam was most relieved. The secretary jumped up and disappeared into the black room also. Dam removed the power plug and stood there waiting. It wasn't long before the phone rang and Dam answered it. It was the people from downstairs wanting to know if the man with the gas mask was alright. That was very nice of them, he thought and he said he was fine, thank you through the gas mask.

Presently there was a knock on the door and a large lady in a pink dress entered the room. "Ee,…ee…er, is this where I learn to meditate?" she asked.

"Oh yes" said Dam and added "the man is very nice, he was so happy to see me. He must be so relieved of stress!"

"H…have you been here long?" asked the lady.

"Oh about one hundred and twenty five years" said Dam. Just then the secretary burst back into the room, she raced over to the phone and rang an angry-lance which was Dam's word for ambulance.

"Electrocution severe" she said and gave the address. She put the phone down and looked at Dam. "Appointment is off," she said, "ring later."

"Oh," said Dam, "is he stressed?"

"Stressed" yelled the woman, "You, Mr Diligent, you electrocuted him!

Oh sorry!" she said turning to the woman. "May I help you?"

"I...I....I'm a nurse" said the woman in pink "c...c..can I h...help?"

"Oh," said Dam "I'm so sorry."

The two ladies and Dam went into the black room. It was very dark. Gradually Dam's eyes grew accustomed to the dark. They all leaned over the figure on the couch. There was a lot of smoke in the room and Dam could just make out the fellows nose.

"Shh, quiet" said the secretary, "he's meditating!" Dam was excited!

He leaned forward to get a better view of somebody who was meditating.

"Oooh" he said as the huge single glass eye of the gas mask hovered over the man in the gloom. Fortunately the man did not open his eyes. The nurse pulled Dam back but he trod on the secretary's foot with his new shoes. She let out a cry and the man opened his eyes.

Dam leaned over him again and said something inaudible. The poor man began screaming and shaking all over, the nurse pulled Dam back and took the man's hand. The man let out another cry and tried to sit up. The secretary was pulling Dam away but not before he had put his hand on the man's shoulder.

"Relax, relax," said Dam, "You are getting sleepy."

"Aagh, argh" said the man as he was forced back down.

The secretary had Dam by the coat tails now. She pulled him back and out of the door.

"We can manage," she said politely and shut the door.

Dam stood there a while not knowing what to do. He turned to go and noticed his electric light cord on the ground in front of the exit door. As he bent down to put it in his bag the door suddenly flew open and collided with his head.

There was a resounding bang as Dam's gas mask was knocked off him.

He slumped to the floor. The angry-lance men seeing Dam flat on the floor tested his pulse and found an extremely faint one. Dam was imbibing incense smoke now and lay there twitching slightly.

They carried him out. At the top of the stairs they were suddenly stopped by the secretary. Dam unfortunately slid off the stretcher and bumped down the stairs ending up in a heap on the next level! His little bag of shopping burst open revealing lots of bars of chocolate. One angry-lance man ran down and propped him up on the handrail, his gas mask hung loosely about his neck.

Then he returned to the electrocuted man in the room.

When they entered they saw a very strange site. The man had blown himself up into a large balloon or rather his skin had formed a large bubble. His face looked most peculiar with two huge transparent cheeks, his blackened charcoal hair and his little beady eyes.

They put him on a stretcher and carried him out. As they passed Dam on the corner of the stairs one of the angry-lance men slipped on a chocolate and the man with the bubbles bounced off the stretcher and landed on the ground in front of Dam. Dam opened his eyes and seeing the meditation man with the swollen face thought he was in the morgue again! He leaned forward when he recognised the little beady eyes looking at him and said,

"My, you do look stressed" and poked the man in the cheek. There was a sudden rush of wind, the man completely collapsed like an empty balloon and his face resumed its normal size. "That's better, just relax" Dam said.

The man groaned as the angry-lance men came and lifted him back on the stretcher. Dam watched them load him into the angry-lance. With the red light flashing on the faces of the onlookers Dam gathered his chocolates, content to eat one as he sat down again on the stairs above the little crowd which had gathered below.

"Arr..ar.. you alright?" came a voice from behind. Dam was a little startled and turned around to see the pale knees and the white legs of the lady in the pink dress as she stood on the stairs above him. Dam chocked. Chocolate had caught in his wind pipe. He tried to talk but nothing happened, suddenly he stopped breathing. He stood up, the gas mask dangling in front of him.

He looked at the lady and gasped for air. The woman seeing what was wrong came down and thumped him on the back with such force he flew into the handrail in front and doubled over it, about to fall off the stairs! The woman grabbed him by the ankles just as he was about to fall and suspended him like a newborn infant in mid-air. With her right hand she made an almighty fist and clobbered Dam fair in the chest. Chocolate sprayed everywhere. She hauled him back over the hand rail and stood him on his feet. "M...M...Mary is my name," she said holding out her gigantic outstretched hand.

"D...D... (hick) Dam Dili..Dilli..gent" said Dam as he took it in his tiny hand and felt its crushing strength.

"How...(hick) ..can I stop (hick) these (hick) hiccc..ups?" he asked.

"Tha....tha...ts e..ea..sy" said Mary. And she grabbed Dam's throat in a claw like grasp.

He stood there unable to move; he did not know what to do. Who was this woman, was she really a nurse or a fanatical female wrestler? Dam's eyes began to bulge, but no "hicks" came out!

"J...j..just a little while l..l...longer" she said. The grip tightened, Dam was turning blue. He was on his knees. Onlookers became concerned and Mary said "J...j..just a sl...sl..ight c..case of the hiccups, f..f..fixed ..soon." She let go. Dam fell flat on his face and didn't move.

"Y…y..you c…can get up now" said Mary. But Dam lay very still. His little bag of shopping still strapped to his back. After sometime Mary rolled him over. "S…s….strange" she said as she felt for his pulse. There was none.

Quick as a flash she planted her lips on Dam's and blew him up like a balloon. Dam's chest rose and fell. After sometime Mary began to pump Dam's chest with her hands. Still no breath or heart beat. Then she sat on Dam's chest and bounced up and down. There was an almighty crack and she cautiously got off.

"He's dead!" said an onlooker. Mary looked worried. She ran up the stairs back to the secretary and rang an angry-lance. On her way back down she slipped at the top of the stairs on chocolate and was launched, legs first at the small crowd which had gathered around Dam. Some saw the high heeled shoes first others saw everything.

Bodies flew everywhere. One man was knocked over the railing, another fell down the stairs. Mary landed flat on her face cushioned by Dam's body.

She groaned and rolled over jabbing her elbow in his stomach. People came about from everywhere. One man had a broken arm, another lay prostrate on the ground floor below. Presently the angry-lance arrived and helped everybody in. Mary came along too as she was a nurse and wanted to help.

Dam never reached the horse-piddle they dropped him off at the morgue. Next morning he woke up. He was in horse-piddle or was he? The man beside him looked blue with cold and really sick.

The man on the other side was his friend, the meditation teacher!

Dam recognised the burnt hair. Dam sat up; his little bag of shopping was beside him so he reached in for some chocolate which was all broken into small pieces. He sat there nibbling for a while casting his gaze about the room.

He looked at his friend and suddenly had an idea.

He reached inside his bag and pulled out the electric lead. Then he wheeled the cooked man over to a power point, plugged the lead in and put the end wires on the fellows head. Nothing happened. The connection wasn't good Dam thought. He stuck the wires in the man's ear but that didn't work either. So Dam lifted the man's arm and put the wires under his arm pit. Suddenly a leg shot up in the air, the man sat bolt upright and opened his eyes.

"Where am I?" he said. To which Dam replied

"You are in Heaven."

Just then the door opened and in walked the man with the rice-pudding skin.

"Eek!" he yelled. "You again, you are both meant to be dead!"

"Both of us?" said the meditation man.

Dam cleared his throat; it still felt a little sore. He remembered now though he still looked a little puzzled.

"What's this?" said the man as he picked up the electric lead.

It was too late; the man's hair left the man's body, it was a wig. His glasses filled with steam and he let out a cry. Dam quickly turned the power off and the man stood there as stiff as a board smelling of burnt rice-pudding. Dam and the meditation man wheeled a stretcher over to him and gently laid him to rest.

He was still alive and mumbling something about dinner. His jaw was trembling so Dam gave him a little piece of chocolate. He put it in the man's mouth it was like mowing the lawn only the other way around. The man's glasses cleared and his eyes opened and began staring at the ceiling.

"That was a hell of a hand shake!" said the meditation man and added, "I've been to Nirvana and back, saw the light and met God himself, I do believe I've been enlightened!" Dam looked at him with a queasy ecclesiastical expression.

The meditation man moved closer his black molten beard and hair clinging to his frazzled skin like someone who had been buried for a while.

"You must be a hell of a good guru" he said. "You teach me please....I'll follow your lead." Dam looked at the exposed wires hanging from the end of it.

"Oh..." said Dam somewhat surprised. He looked down at the rice-pudding man who wasn't swallowing his chocolate properly.

"I keep getting the hiccups, I'm not good at relaxing...very stressed," said Dam humbly.

"Hiccups, nonsense, got nothing to do with stress, what you need is confidence" said the meditation man. He looked down at the man on the stretcher and said, "He looks like he's seen a few ghosts!"

"Confidence is what you need" he continued as he slapped Dam on the back so hard he nearly fell over. "Why you've given me confidence, makes one live a lot longer, happy to be alive!"

The rice-pudding man groaned and moved an arm. The meditation man lifted his hand and bit one of the man's fingers. Nothing happened.

"I'll try some pressure points" he said as he began poking the man in the stomach and in the eyes. "You've done your work on this chap too" he continued, "though he doesn't look enlightened. Help me sit him up and we'll see what's cooking."

Dam got behind him and pushed him up into a sitting position, where he slumped forward then sideways, then fell onto the floor like rice-pudding.

"Oops," said the meditation man as the man spread out. He and Dam bent down and took hold of an arm and tried to heave him back up on the bed. But he sagged everywhere. It was no good, he slipped off and fell face down on the cold white tiles again. He let out a groan and lay still.

"He needs some of this" said Dam pointing to the electric cord.

"Oh yes indeed," cried the meditation man and added, "Me too!" Dam and the meditation man dragged rice-pudding man over to the electric lead and plugged him in by placing it under the man's arms. Nothing happened!

"The connection isn't too good" said Dam.

Just as the meditation man crouched down to adjust the connection two people entered the room. Both had long white robes on and Dam thought that if they had wings they would have looked like angels.

"What's going on?" said one of them "Henry are you alright?" Both men knelt down beside the rice-pudding man and felt his pulse.

Two hundred and forty volts of pulse! Both men began shooting blue sparks and the meditation man began hopping about clapping! "Oh wow!" he said as three figures in white robes lay flat on the floor. Suddenly the rice-pudding man sat up and said, "I think I've been to heaven and back!"

"Brilliant!" said the meditation man slapping Dam on the back,

"You're a genius!"

Dam looked up at him from down on the floor next to the power point.

He was about to say next please instead he said nothing and looked at the white walls, the neon lights and the bodies on the floor and on the stretchers. Then the thought that he might be able to electrocute them all entered his head, the thought that they may all wake up and live was alive in his mind!

"Wheel them up!" he said at last.

"What?" said the meditation man.

"Wheel them up and we will see if any of them are sleeping." The meditation man began at the end of the room and brought the first dead body up to the power point.

"A little tickle under the arm" said Dam as he gently put the naked wires under the person's arm and turned the power on. The first was a very old lady and immediately a leg shot into the air then her eyes opened and she cried, "George, I told you not to do that!"

Next was a middle aged man; he just about leapt off the bed! In no time at all the empty stretchers were stacked in the corner as many people in white robes, smelling of great aunt's washing powder stood around.

"Last two" said Dam as he approached the two assistants on the ground.

Soon they too were standing about talking about their wonderful dreams and feelings of great peace.

"This calls for a celebration." said the meditation man. So they all walked out in single file and began to float down the street. Most were bare footed as they entered the pub and ordered champagne.

"We've all come back from the dead" they told the barman "and some of us have been enlightened!" With that the little old lady sprang up on a table and began lifting up her legs and dancing.

"I always wanted to be a famous dancer!" she said.

Dam woke up. He was still in the church. The bells were still ringing though all was dark. He was cold and stiff. He climbed to his feet bumping his head on a polished pew. He sat there a while remembering his dream. His little bag of shopping was by his side and he stretched and stood up.

Out in the street he noticed a sign, it read. "Insure yourself for a longer life." Dam kept walking. It was night, the street lights above were like huge planets down close. There were no stars.

Presently he heard singing; then a pedestrian crossing with the lights on red. The singing grew louder as down the road came forty people with bare feet all dressed in white and all bearing candles. They passed in front of him still singing like the wind in pine trees.

Out in front was a little old lady dancing, ringing a bell and following on behind was a man with burnt hair and beard, he was dressed in dark clothes and seemed to be carrying a large cross! Dam blinked as the traffic lights changed. Other people came towards him, young faces looking through him.

People left his side of the curb but Dam just stood there his mind was moving through galaxies of change. He tightened his grasp on his little bag of shopping and stepped onto the road. Just then there was a loud screeching sound as a car came so close to Dam's knees and stopped. He received a terrible shock and quickly walked on. The driver of the car leaned out the window and said,

"You're the luckiest man alive." Dam's heart began to pound. He looked at the driver it was the rice-pudding man with his two assistants.

When Dam reached the other side of the road he found he had a terrible bout of hiccups.

Dam Locks His Keys in the Shed

Dam had a shed as strong as a safe. He had spent a lot of time building it and making it strong. It had double walls and three big locks on the door.

"Nobody knows that the roof is hinged and lifts up" he said. Knowing that the locks were all show especially if one knew that the roof lifted up.

Unfortunately for Dam late one evening he left the keys inside the shed and locked the door. But Dam being diligent knew he could climb in through the roof to get them.

He went and found a ladder and climbed up one side of the shed where he could lift the roof up and prop it open with a stick. He hauled himself over the wall and jumped inside but collected the stick when he jumped down and unfortunately for Dam his jacket caught at the back on one of the hooks he'd made to secure the roof on the inside in case of strong wind. The roof slammed down with a terrific bang and jammed shut! He had trapped himself in his own shed!

Dam hung there by his jacket suspended from the wall. He tried pushing himself up with his feet but there were no foot holds. He tried to grasp the top of the wall but it was too far above him. Dam was in the dark, one could hear him banging about like a frog in a tin.

Fortunately for Dam he was hanging near his tools and fortunately for Dam he had night seeing eyes. In a twinkling he found a screw driver and began to unscrew one of the massive hinges on the door. It soon fell away and a flood of dim light filled the blackness through the screw holes. Now at least he had a foot hold. He placed his foot between the door and the door jam and stood up as best he could as his foot was being forced into the narrow opening.

With great difficulty he freed his jacket and left it hanging there for as he let go his foot became jammed and he was left, once again, though a little lower to the floor, suspended on the wall, this time by his foot! Fortunately he could now undo the other hinge which he did quite quickly though his foot was very sore. Dam fell to the floor he was free.

But alas the door still did not want to open. He had a bad pain in his neck after hitting the floor with one leg and his head had to be kept to one side.

He decided it was too painful and needed to be fixed so he began to straighten his head by putting the elbow which was on the same side as his head, on his temple and pulled himself up with the other hand on the hook where his jacket was so he suspended himself again for a short time. Fortunately for Dam his neck crunched back into place and luckily he landed on his feet though one of those was still a quite sore. He hobbled over to the other hinge and began to undo it. Would he ever get out he wondered?

Just then a dream sequence faded across his mind where he saw himself in a cave with a steel box. The box had a small hole in it at head height.

Dam walked up to it and looked in. To Dam's surprise there was another person in the box sitting next to a candle. The person rose and came over to Dam and poked him in the eye through the hole!

Dam woke up. He was still in the shed. He began to think again. Was the man in the steel box the butcher who had short changed him the other day?

Dam wondered what the butcher would do to get out of a steel box in a cave.

He finally decided not to think too much about silly things and concentrate on getting out. But he couldn't stop thinking and he wondered about his thought. Was the steel box a fridge? Was the butcher trying to give him advice about how to get out? Dam rubbed his eye and decided the butcher had cut his finger and had cursed Dam to lock himself in his shed and then short-changed him! Dam had trouble concentrating, he decided at that moment, rather than a poke in the eye with a finger what he really needed was a hand!

Night was falling and he felt for the screws on the third hinge. As he was feeling for the hinge a small whispering sound came to Dam's ears. It grew louder and louder until he realised the neighbours were having an argument.

No, it seemed closer than that. Then all of a sudden the door of the shed was violently shaken and a loud voice yelled, "Oo ees een me sheed?!" Dam mistook the words for "could you get out of my bed!"

Dam was shocked to think that the whole shed was shaking because of their raised voices in the bedroom! Finally he realised there was somebody outside and he put his eye up to the crack in the door and peeped out. At that moment another eye came up to meet his. Dam quickly poked it first, thinking it was the butcher!

"Owe!" There was a loud cry from outside then suddenly the door flew open and Dam was blinded by a powerful torch light. He could vaguely work out the figure of his next-door neighbour.

"You!" the man said holding his eye, "A've cought oo steelin in me sheed!"

"Your shed!" cried Dam, "but it's mine!"

"Oh no, no, no, no, snizent" Dam looked around; well it was so similar....

"Oh no!" he said to himself "I am so sorry." he said to the man.

"I have a shed just the same!" Dam was feeling very stupid to say the least!

"Look!" said the man who was beginning to sound like the butcher "Zee walls af bent een." Dam could see that the top of the walls had buckled and the walls were squashed in!

"Oove ruined me sheed!" said the man as he poked poor Dam in the eye. Dam's neck went out again, his head to the side! The man stormed off holding his eye and whimpering something about "aye loos me aye n inges, oowe!"

Dam thought it must have been when he was straightening his neck that he'd buckled the walls. There wasn't much he could do except apologise to the man and go back home.

As soon as he arrived home he looked at himself sideways in the mirror. Eventually he said to himself,

"Thank heavens for neighbours, I could have been locked in there for weeks!"

Dam Plants an Orange Tree

The weather had been very dry. The leaves were crisp on the ground.

Dam watched the sky in the hope of rain because he'd bought an orange tree and planted it in good soil down the slope from his house. He had collected a large pile of sticks next to it and intended to set fire to the sticks when conditions were right so he could put the ash on the tree to help it grow.

In the meantime he was fast at work building a hydraulic powered bicycle which worked on the principle of using the hollow frame of the bike as an air compression chamber.

He had been working on it for ten years and it was nearly finished. The oil pump charging system however needed a special lever and he remembered using the same shaped piece of metal in the cement foundation he'd made for his new room two days before.

Dam couldn't make another lever so out of desperation he went to work with a sledge hammer and broke up his new floor in order to find the special part. After about three hours he came across the piece of metal, worked it free and spent another three hours cleaning the cement off it.

He went back to his shed, lever in hand and tried it out on his bicycle which was a new invention and had become a masterpiece of monumental engineering. Dam had a wonderful eye for engineering principles and the part fitted snugly and performed well.

Excitedly he climbed up onto it for its first test run.

One half turn of the pedal and Dam shot forward and crashed into a tree. A small problem with the steering he said, which he had forgotten to install!

With a sore foot he set about repairing the concrete foundation, mixing more cement and smoothing it over until it looked new. When he was finishing he felt a drop of rain and looking up saw a large black cloud growing darker by the minute. He quickly hobbled and fetched some newspaper and plastic to cover the wet cement.

As he watched the sky, rain began to fall and soon the ground was wet. Dam hobbled and hopped down to his pile of sticks and lit all around the edge of it.

The rain came down and the flames roared up. Soon a huge blaze was writhing about in the slight breeze. The flame was four meters high and stretched its fiery fingers right across to his little orange tree and frazzled it in seconds!

Dam could only watch in horror as his little tree withered and then burst into flames. The fire was so hot it burnt the grass all around.

Dam stood there in the rain and watched the rain-drops hissing and spitting in the fire. Fortunately the rain was heavy enough to put out the grass-fire but the sticks kept burning.

When the fire was out Dam hobbled up the hill, his foot still sore. At least he'd produced a large pile of ash and fixed his bicycle.

He checked the wet cement and it was safe and dry. That night it rained and it poured, little rivulets started up everywhere. He spent his evening designing some steering for his bicycle, it was a difficult task.

As he slept he had a dream that his little orange tree grew very tall and produced lots of hydraulic powered bicycles with perfect steering instead of fruit! He inspected the fruit carefully in order to understand the principle of the steering. He woke early the next morning and set about redesigning the steering but try as he might he couldn't make the part which he needed.

His thoughts began to wander and he suddenly remembered seeing the exact part in amongst the scrap metal of the same foundation he'd remade the day before! In no time at all he smashed up the concrete again but couldn't find the part.

He then smashed up the whole foundation into small pieces. But still he could not find it!

Then Dam remembered it wasn't in the foundation at all, it was in one of his boxes of scrap metal in the shed! He went to his shed and began to sort through all the piles of metal. Eventually he found it however it was slightly different to what he had imagined. He set about trying to fit it into his creation. More pieces were needed and the idea still did not work.

After lunch he repaired the concrete foundation again taking care to smooth it over carefully and make it look like it was new. His bicycle tormented him and he went to his boxes of scrap metal to look for ideas.

Several days passed and still his creation had no steering. Eventually he made something which needed a test run so he climbed aboard his hydraulic powered super-bicycle and pointed it downhill. As he worked the steering and began to pick up speed the thought hit him that the contraption had no brakes! The steering was very awkward and sluggish and he soon found himself bumping over bumps and banging into logs. Then he ran straight over his orange tree!

He ended up in a pile of bushes all scratched with a damaged foot again.

He tried pushing the bike back up hill but only managed a few steps as it was so heavy! He stopped next to his little orange tree which was squashed and broken.

He stood above his bicycle with his sore foot and try as he might he simply couldn't lift the bike back up onto its wheels. He had lost his strength. He left it there saying he'd come back and get it when his foot was better.

It was some years later when he returned. And to his joy he found a large orange tree laden with fruit beside his old invention. He cleared the grass away from the bicycle and soon realised it was too rusty to be of any use. So he sat on the back wheel and ate some oranges. Whenever the orange tree was in fruit he'd go down and sit on the bike in the shade of the tree and eat fresh oranges.

He tried not to think of his hydraulic powered bicycle.

He thought rather about the oranges and how the rusting metal of the bike was feeding the tree. The oranges were far sweeter than the bicycle's complicated engineering problems.

Then one day he looked down at the orange in his hand and saw in minute detail the engineering needed for fixing the steering.

He uncovered the bike and began pushing the rusty contraption up the hill. After some minor adjustments and lots of oil he realised that it needed a particular shaped piece of metal. He went into his shed and began rummaging through his boxes of scrap metal. Search as he might he could not find the part. Then he remembered seeing the very thing he needed and realised it was buried in the concrete foundation of the room he'd built all those years ago.

Dam Plays Golf

One day Dam woke early. He felt full of life and energy. He bounded out of bed and hardly looked at the shirt he put on, it just seemed to be there in the right place. Sometimes he became horribly tangled in his clothes. They were either inside-out or he put his head in the wrong hole. This morning however his arm went in the right hole for his arm and his head went in the right hole for his head. His socks and trousers were no trouble at all to put on. He was dressed and ready in seconds.

"Nothing can go wrong today," he said as he miraculously found his shoes exactly where he had left them.

Dam looked out the window the sun was just beginning to lift the sky and the birds were calling.

Today I shall play golf with my friend, he said as he went into the kitchen to find some food. Miraculously he found some food in a cupboard just where he'd left it the day before. Things were going well for him this morning!

Dam lived alone, alone that is, except for his friend who was Dam himself.

He would spend ages talking to himself - his "friend" as he called him.

"How are you this morning?" He'd say to himself at the kitchen table,

"Oh I'm great thank you."

"Want to play golf?" he questioned,

"Oh yes," said Dam "I bet you loose and I win"

"Oh ho ho," he said "you've never won against me yet!" Silence, he was wondering when he last played golf with himself. He couldn't remember.

"You win, I'll eat my hat!" One of Dam's eyes suddenly closed and opened automatically.

Dam had all the things he liked to eat for breakfast. Chocolate, rice pudding and twelve eggs. He washed it all down with lemonade and tomato sauce.

He packed a lunch of sardines and chocolate and found his old straw hat.

He was ready and stood at the doorway of his house and looked out over the countryside.

"Which way shall we play golf today?" he asked himself. "North, south, east of west? If I travel east into the sun I won't get lost" he answered.

He went out to his garden shed and found two golf balls and three clubs.

The large club he had made from the root of a cherry tree, he used it in his garden to smash up clods of dirt. The chipper he made out of an old outboard motor propeller. He had used it to chip weeds with and the putter he had made from a slab of iron he'd used as a lever for extracting tree stumps.

The heavier the better he said. He took all these out onto his front lawn and made a little support for the ball out of a little clod of clay.

He was ready. Pushing back his hat and looking into the sun he belted the ball as hard as he could. It completely disappeared. Somewhere in the distance Dam heard the sound of a smashing window.

"Well I'll be," he said to himself. "See you've lost already!"

"Oh no I haven't," he answered himself and added, "Watch this!"

Dam muttered under his breath, "this guy thinks I haven't got any balls."

Dam did not reply, he went to his shed and found another ball, gave it a polish and placed it carefully on the ground.

He put the other ball on a little clod of clay and belted it. This time he saw it skew sideways terribly and hit a tree. It then flew over his head and smashed a window in his kitchen.

"Damn!" said Dam as he pushed his hat back, picked up his clubs and stormed into the kitchen. It took him a long time to find the ball for it was hiding in the hole in the sink.

"Hole in one," he said to himself laughing. He put his chipper in the sink and suddenly bashed at the ball which rolled back in the hole. It was sometime after that he worked out how to hit it out of the hole in his sink. He put it in a spoon and banged the other end of the spoon and out it popped out onto the bench.

Dam stood on his bench top amongst the washing up and took out his large cherry tree root club. He took his golf seriously. There was a small opening on the left side of the window. If he could to tap the ball slightly on the right side it should jump neatly out the window.

As he drew the club back something over-came him and he excitedly swung too hard. There was a loud smash as he missed the ball and smashed many of his plates!

It wasn't his eye that was wrong, it was the fact that in the final swing he'd lost all sense of precaution and hit the ball as hard as he could! It was a problem he had had for a long time. He'd sought medical advice about this condition and found that other people had "Ballsy" as well. The symptoms varied from a mad ball-frenzy which involved the feet and the hands, to guarding a hitting object such as a stick or a bat, anything the sufferer could grasp and potentially use uncontrollably to hit the nearest ball. Many people with both symptoms have been known to travel great distances just to get relief from hitting a ball.

The badly afflicted I am told, begin to believe that balls have a consciousness because they are round and that they insight people to violence and competition which is like comparing them to a bad dream or a potentially harmful meal.

Dam was still standing on his kitchen bench, heavily breathing after the stroke and looking at the ball which had been terrified and bounced out and down onto the kitchen floor. He kept his eye on it as he climbed down as though it may move again without any warning.

It was his friend's turn to hit the ball. His friend suffered from the opposite symptoms to Ballsy and tended to hit the ball too softly! He tried again and after sometime he managed to putt the ball out of the kitchen and into the hall-way. He opened the door and decided to use his long-iron to get the ball on its way. Aunt Betsy was looking down on him from the wall. She had nothing to do with golf so Dam didn't mind her watching. Now she was caged in an ancient photograph which was eaten away at the edges by age and faded in the eyes by having them open all the time.

Dam's swing tore the photograph off the wall and smashed the ball to the end of the hallway where it buried itself in the clock and started the alarm ringing! The club finished embedded in the wall. A small cloud of plaster dusted down onto the floor.

It was no good the clock was totally distressed and had almost completely swallowed the ball! Dam took out his putter and prised the clock off the wall.

It fell down with a ringing-clang. Taking his club his friend wacked it outside where it danced on the lawn some distance away and stopped ringing.

The ball however did not emerge. Dam lifted his hat back and said,

"This isn't much fun!" As he descended the stairs on to the lawn, his eyes kept fiercely watching the remains of the clock hoping that the ball would see him coming and automatically roll out of it, but it didn't.

Taking his club he pushed his hat back and looked up at the sun. Dam liked a challenge. There was a loud clang as he launched the clock across the garden in the direction of the other ball. Dam's game involved two balls.

He would smash one any direction as hard as he could then "tap" the other one as close to the other as he could.

Dam kept his eye on the clock as he wound his body up for the swing.

"Clang!" The clock landed high up in a tree and stayed there! Undaunted Dam began throwing his golf clubs up at it. A few moments later he looked around and found there were no more clubs to throw as they were all stuck in the tree.

Dam said, "Damn, you win," as he went and fetched his ladder.

The ladder unlike Dam was old and rickety. He soon had it balanced precariously on a limb of the tree. As he was working his way along a branch with his legs on either side a gentle breeze blew the top of the tree where the clock was and much to Dam's delight the golf ball came bounding down the branches and landed on the ground. Two clubs slithered out of the tree also but the chipper remained well stuck a fair way above him. Dam climbed up the trunk then along another thinner branch and out onto an even thinner limb where he hoped he could reach some leaves of the branch above where the club was. As he stood on one leg - on tippy-toes, he stretched out his fingers, straining to reach the lowest leaves when a gentle breeze moved the tree and the chipper slid out and down to the ground.

Much relieved Dam climbed down and pushing his hat back he fetched his largest club. Looking east he belted the balls and watched them disappear through the trees. He hoped both balls had jumped the trees and landed in the paddock next door. He picked up his lunch and marched off through the bush determined to find his balls.

"Already I am four strokes behind you" he said to himself. "Watch me though, I'll catch up!"

He hadn't walked far when, believe it or not, he came upon a small stream and in that stream gleaming white was a golf ball.

"Arh ha, I've found you" said Dam talking to his ball. Quick as a flash he took his shirt off and gripping his chipper, plunged in.

Fortunately the creek was not too deep as he bent down with his head under the water and began to take aim at the ball with his putter. He hit once and it rolled a meter. The current caught it and rolled it a lot more. Dam waded along as best he could. Occasionally dipping his head beneath to watch where the ball was going for it was on its way down-stream. Dam lifted his knees high then all of a sudden he fell down into deep water. Peering below he found his ball had settled in some leaves at the bottom of the pool. He dived down and took a swing at it but missed. Suddenly he realised he couldn't get back to the surface as his putter was so heavy. He stuck it in the mud and came up for air then dived down again and began walking along the bottom with the putter holding him down. He walked up the bank huffing and puffing and sat on a stone for a little moment to catch his breath. He took his light-weight chipper and plunged back in. Dam was soon surrounded by dense mud and he couldn't see a thing. He came up for air and tried again. But no matter how hard he tried, he could not get his bottom to stay under the water because his hands were holding the club.

"This is no good," he said at last as he emerged from the pool and sat on the bank. After some thought he fetched his shoes and socks. He undid the shoe laces and filled each sock with rocks. Then he tied the socks to his feet and dragged himself over to the pool. Slowly he began to submerge, deeper and deeper he went with his bottom the right way up. He found his ball, it was still in the mud waiting for him.

"I've got you now" he said as he took another deep breath and dived down. Dam was indeed a masterful player of golf. In no time at all the ball was close to the edge of the stream and Dam was clambering along after it with his socks full of rocks. A final tap and the ball leapt up onto the bank where it gleamed again in the bright sunshine.

He left it there and emptied the rocks from his socks. He then dressed and went looking for his other ball. He spent a long time looking and after some time grew hungry and sat down under a shady tree to eat his lunch and dry his socks.

"Ball, ball where are you, ball" he'd even made up a little song about his balls; it went like this, "Ball, ball where are you, balls? I call and I call for my little white balls, they are not so small, after all they're only balls."

He couldn't think of anything else to add to that so he started singing it again. As he was eating his sardines he noticed a lizard eating ants. Dam tossed it a piece of sardine and it poked its tongue out at him.

"Oh that's nice" said Dam and added "Do you know where my ball is?"

The lizard sat up and looked at Dam then bobbed its head frantically and waved.

Dam stopped chewing as the lizard ran off with Dam close behind. And there under a tuft of grass was the golf ball. Dam excitedly finished his lunch and reached for his clubs. Taking aim with his bent-propeller-blade chipper he chipped it over the grass in the direction of the other ball. Now the two balls were united and Dam resumed the game of golf with himself.

"I'm better than you" he said to himself.

"No I'm better than you, ask the lizard!"

"I can hit my ball harder ask the clock."

Dam began to chip the ball at an object and then say "See how close you can get to my ball," the one closest to the object has to aim at the other person's ball. Dam got out his putter and aimed at the other ball. "If I hit your ball I win." he said, but he missed.

The chase was on. Over hill and down gullies the two balls chased each other.

"Oh ho ho, I'll get you now," he said, but he missed. Dam had completely forgotten which ball was which. That didn't seem to matter for if one ball hit the other, that ball won!

"Ball, ball where are my balls...is my ball!" he corrected himself with a chuckle. For there was something about balls which made him forget things.

He spied a tree in the distance and took out his tree-root club.

Wack! One ball rocketed towards the tree, followed closely by the other.

Dam walked up to the tree and found the first ball but not the second.

All he found was a hole in the ground where the ball was supposed to be.

He thought it looked like a snake hole!

"Oh dear me!" he said to himself. "I think I've got a hole in one!"

"No, no, no" came the retort. "You weren't aiming for that hole!"

"How do you know I wasn't?"

"You can't get your ball back though, can you?"

Dam scratched his chin, pushed his hat back and peered into the hole. It was round and deep just the sort of hole a golf ball or a snake would like!

"Now I've definitely won," he said concluding that he had purposefully hit the ball into the hole.

"My game," he sighed.

Looking up at the sky he decided he'd had enough golf for one day and began to chip the remaining ball along the bumpy path towards home singing his song,

"Ball, ball where are my balls? I call and I call, for my little balls. They aren't too small…." He'd forgotten the rest!

Not much happened on the way home. He didn't hit the ball really hard and wasn't really aiming at anything. All he could think about was his ball and the snake talking together.

When he came to the forest he took out his putter and tapped the ball through the trees. Then he came to his front lawn and to his amazement found his clock on the ground, it was all broken! He looked at it twice for he'd completely forgotten about it! Then he found his ladder half way up a tree. Dam pushed his hat back and scratched his head. Who could have done this?! Had he done that?

As he bent down to pick up his only ball he said to it,

"Argh you poor thing, a hiding today! At least you're not down a nasty old snake hole. And just for you," he said "I'm going to make sure you don't get lost, you may have lost the game but the other ball is lost for ever!" With that he put it in his pocket.

He went up the steps to the front door and found somebody had opened it! Maybe they were still inside! He took out his putter and went in slowly, bending low. He searched every room fully expecting to find somebody.

Dam was horrified to find his house wrecked! Aunt Betsy was still on the floor. She looked like she had been hit by a golf club! And in the kitchen there were plates and dishes all smashed up all over the floor! And somebody had smashed a window! Who could have done this he said!

After he'd cleaned up all the mess he pushed his hat back and made a cup of tea. Then he took the golf ball out of his pocket and put it in the middle of the table and said,

"You know what I think…. we won! But I'm certainly not going to eat my hat!"

He reached up to push his hat back again but his hat was not there! He poured himself a cup of tea but the water had no tea in it! He opened the top of the kettle. Somebody had put his hat in the kettle!

Dam Plays Soccer, Again!

Dam as a young man, you may not be surprised, was obsessed with his balls. The larger the better, the bouncier the better. He was a born trickster and would intrigue people in the street by carrying his two balls on his shoulders and bouncing them alternately on his knees and then his feet. He was so adept at tapping them from one side of his body to the other that people would not look where they were going and bang into obstacles just watching him.

He could run along the street and juggle his balls from his shoulders to his feet then to his knees as he went. He would gather speed and looked like some kind of machine. He was well known around town as being the man who ran on two balls.

Dam really wasn't human, he was a phenomena. In a soccer match he was unbeatable and once he had the ball a goal was assured. Consequently the other players tried hard never to let the ball get near him. He could kick a ball with one leg while holding it still with the big toe of the other foot and by moving the ball around and around he could, with a single leg, ride it into the goal posts!

If the other side came to kick the ball away from underneath him he merely changed legs and left them far behind. Dam Diligent was dynamite and dangerous!

Single-footedly he took his team to the greatest heights of world soccer.

His name was quite famous, they called him "Dam Dili-dangerous."

Over the years he devised all sorts of odd ideas which were to challenge the old laws of the game. One such idea was to attach a string to the ball and grip it with his toes and swing it around his head before releasing it with incredible force at the opponent's goal keeper.

He had a healthy disregard for goalies and often knocked them out with the force of his "bare-foot-lightning" kicks as he called them and true, they were virtually unstoppable!

Referees wore helmets when Dam played for he could kick the ball or head it with such force his balls were dangerous. Holes were torn in nets from his lightning kicks. They were as hard to stop as freight trains and no man could stand in their way!

The legend of "Dam Diligent's Dangerous Legs" spread far and wide, he was toe-tally absorbed by the game and always had a trick up his leg. Not only could Dam ride balls past goalies he could run like a cheetah and jump like an impala. He was hard to see at the best of times as he was often just a blur.

Dam's team soon became famous and rose up from nowhere to confront the greatest soccer players in the world who lived in other countries overseas. Dam's team from his Australian outback country town was rapidly rising to stardom and Dam was its greatest player by far. They won all the trophies they could win and were soon on their way to play the greatest team in the world.

One day as Dam was practicing with his two balls he suddenly had a great idea, in fact he had two great ideas at once. The first was to glue springs all over his bald head to assist with header shots and the second was to get another leg stitched on. He rode his two balls to the horse-piddle (hospital) as quickly as he could, flying around corners and through red lights. Keeping up with cars on the highway was easy.

At the horse-piddle Dam was lucky to find a few spare legs for sale.

They had just come in and were quite fresh and cheap. He arranged a time for the operation and was back early next morning. He chose a nice leg that fitted perfectly and though it was a little unhairy and smooth, unlike his other two legs and a bit squeaky at first, after a little practice it seemed to work quite well.

Dam tried hard with his extra leg and after only a short while was mounting obstacles and juggling three balls in a blur of splendour. So fast were his three feet that wrestling a ball from him was an impossible feat and with fifteen toes all demonically dexterous it was damn difficult to even see the ball at times.

Dam developed a method of kicking the ball by gripping it with his two outside feet, throwing it in the air and kicking it with his middle leg. This was positively deadly and as accurate as a snipers bullet especially as he could kick it by spinning backwards in mid-air!

He was a true master but that was not all. Dam glued valve springs to his bald head!

With these he could do headers from one end of the field to the other and it wasn't long before these became deadly accurate as well!

The time had come for the final showdown with the world's best soccer team and Dam, for he was really a one and a half man soccer team. The stadium was packed with screaming fans and as Dam waltzed on to the field many people laughed at him as he was over eighty years old!

The springs on his scalp gleamed in the sunlight and Dam spread his legs a little to reveal his hidden weapon. He flexed his third leg.

The whistle blew and the ball was kicked far over his head. He bided his time and waited for his moment to strike. It wasn't long before the ball made its way to him and he headed it straight for the goal. But unfortunately for Dam it hit the goal post and bounced all the way back down the field and went into the wrong goal!

One nil! The crowd laughed and cheered they'd never seen such a funny thing. This made Dam quite angry and he decided to chase the ball to get the game rolling.

The following incident was recorded in slow-motion by the television cameras covering the game. The footage showed a white streak descend on the ball and before any of the other players knew what was happening Dam was upon them with his three legs and highly sprung bald head.

He did a complicated triple roll-over and slammed the ball upside down with his extra leg. The ball rocketed off and scored a direct hit in the goalies stomach carrying him aloft and into the back of the net!

But Dam was hurt. Something terribly wrong had happened and as the television cameras later revealed Dam's middle leg had become horribly entwined with his other legs and had dislocated because of the tremendous force he'd used to kick the ball. Dam's extra leg had flown up and become stuck in his teeth! He was hastily carried from the field and admitted to horse-piddle with severe foot and mouth disease.

Unfortunately Dam's team lost the game and the other team's goalie was also admitted to the same horse-piddle and the poor man balled all the way!

Dam looked across the room at him in the bed opposite. He wanted to apologise but he couldn't speak as his lips had swollen to the size of soccer balls!

His extra leg lay before him wrapped in bandages. Poor Dam could only shake his head from side to side which made his springs wobble.

Dam apologised to the goalie and swore to himself that he'd never play with his balls again. It was no longer his goal in life to be a trickster with an extra leg.

Over the weeks Dam's lips deflated and he decided to have his extra leg removed.

After they cut it off the soccer people put it in a large glass bottle in a glass case in what they called the "Soccer Hall of Fame." Dam's ability had become a leg-end after all!

Dam and the Dragon

One day Dam was out in the warm sun sitting on a book reading a piece of wood. He was remembering a tale about a farmer's wife who had died and then returned to the milking shed in the reincarnated form of his best milking cow. The story however became very boring for Dam when the book began to describe the farmer's feelings as he stood there staring into the cow's eyes.

At that point a very large flying insect flew abruptly into Dam's face.

The insect fell to the ground unfurled itself and began to clean its wings with its back legs.

"Well," said Dam leaning down, "what sort of an insect are you?"

The creature looked much like a dragon-fly. It may have been a *Rapid takeoffikus,* or *Long bigeye* of the family "Can't Find My Way Home." The dragon-fly turned to him and said in a very thin little voice,

"Long Big Eye, that I am or "Short Legs" for short and you must be Dam?"

Dam nearly fell off his book; he stooped down and had a closer look at Big Eye. Dam began to think to himself that the creature was only a dumb creature and that it was he who was hearing things.

At that moment the insect flew off the ground and landed on the tip of Dam's huge nose, clung on tightly and with its tail squirted some fluid up into one of Dam's nostrils and then the other. Dam got such a shock he smashed himself in the face and immediately killed the insect which spiralled down dead to the ground. Dam's nose began to furiously throb and twist one way and then the other. Indeed it began to bend and shake. He gripped it and looked around for something to blow it on. He found one leaf but that was too small then he found another but that was too large, he found another but that wasn't right either so he took off his shirt and blew his nose on that.

His nose had settled down and Dam's little voice stopped. And as he bent down to pick up his book he looked at the insect on the ground and decided to bury it.

"Poor thing," he said to himself, "I'll have to bury it." As he stooped down to pick it up it moved slightly so Dam picked it up in his hand.

"Ahh," came the voice to him again. He listened to it but there were no more sounds. He picked up his book and with the insect in the other hand began to walk home.

He began to talk to himself about the insect when he heard it say,

"Argh, you've injured me and I may die if you don't give me a drink of water and you've bent my wind-pipe." Dam stopped and looked at the creature. It did look rather bent. So he straightened it and put it on his shoulder. It looked up at Dam's massive body moving so slowly through space.

"Where are you going?" it said in a soft little voice and Dam replied,

"To get you a drink." After some moments the voice came back to him and said,

"And what will you achieve from all this" and Dam answered.

"I will heal you!"

He put the insect on the table and poured some water next to it. The insect lay there for a while then crawled over to the water and had a drink.

Next it was drowning or swimming through the water. Dam came in close with his giant-earth eyes and saw that it was swimming on its back looking up at him. Suddenly he was sure he heard it say,

"If you do something for me, I will do something for you."

"Oh!" said Dam and thought a while, then said,

"What is your wish?"

"You know what your wish is, go and look in the mirror and you'll see what kind of a wish you have." Dam went and looked in the mirror but he did not see himself, instead he saw what looked like a Dragon. Dam looked a second time and felt his scales.

He opened his mouth and fire came out. He went back to the insect and whispered.

"What on earth have you done to me, I'm a dragon?" The insect then stood up and transformed into a large female Dragon.

"Soo pleased to meet you" said Dam.

Dam Feeds his Trees

Early one morning well before the sun had risen Dam looked at the sky.

He had bought some seed a long time ago and had waited weeks for the right time to spread it under his orange trees in the orchard. He had little time anyway as his other commitments kept him very busy far into the night. He had found that oranges gave him the energy he needed for he would rise early in the mornings as his time was precious.

This day it looked like rain so he decided to quickly spread the seed.

He lit a fire and began to boil half a bucket of water, next he added a lot of sugar, as much as he had left after eating most of it for breakfast. He waited for it to cool then added the seed and a special powder which was apparently dried leguminous-nitrogen-fixing bacteria. The sugar would make the powder stick to the seed he was told.

He went outside and smelt the air, his orange trees were in full blossom and he could taste the perfume. As he was spreading his treated leguminous-nitrogen-fixing bacteria seed he suddenly thought that the bacteria may penetrate his skin and begin to grow within him. He held his breath and tried not to inhale the fine dust into his lungs.

After he'd walked around his twenty trees he let out his breath.

And thereafter there was an enormous inrush of air that caught an unsuspecting bee which Dam was sure he swallowed. Luckily he was not stung or so he thought!

Exactly three weeks after that day Dam began to grow funny dangling lumps all over his body! The little lumps began to appear first on his chin then under his arms! He felt his chest and found that two lumps were distressingly large and distinctly prominent in an embarrassingly obvious position. As the lumps grew he began to feel like an orange tree in full fruit! And as he walked he felt like an orange tree swaying in the wind!

He decided that he was not only blossoming but his body was growing leguminous-nitrogen-fixing bacteria! He looked at his toes, they were growing thinner and longer like roots! The lumps on his body began to grow larger and actually seemed to be ripening as they were turning an orange colour!

He became exceedingly embarrassed when in public and began to go out less and less. As his lumps grew he noticed they became covered in little dimples. That wasn't so bad it was shaving in between them all which took such a long time!

One day he was out shopping when suddenly one of them fell off and rolled along the floor. He quickly put it in his shopping trolley. At the check-out the lady picked it up and examined it carefully.

"Did you buy this here?" she asked. Dam looked embarrassed and said that he had grown it himself for he always told the truth.

"Do you grow commercially?" she asked.

"When I have enough" Dam replied. Over the next few weeks many of his oranges fell off. He studied them under a microscope and found they had seeds and juice just like a real oranges! He buried himself in books and watched his hair go white. Then one day he noticed that bees were attracted to his hair!

"Perhaps I am in flower?" he said laughingly.

Over the next few months the lumps began to grow again! And the two on his chest became huge!

He went back to his books and waited for himself to mature. He harvested his lumps and began to sell them to the shops. Everybody said they were delicious! He bought more nitrogen-fixing-bacteria powder and mixed it into his breakfast. He studied his lumps every day. The next time he was in fruit and his two big lumps matured and fell off he took them to an agricultural show and submitted them as huge fruit.

He was photographed in the local paper and became quite famous. The fruit ended up in a museum. He was well known for growing the largest fruit in the area and many other orange farmers wanted to know his secret.

Then one day he saw a new type of banana tree with giant bananas.

Dam loved bananas so he bought a plant. That was the last time anybody saw Dam in a public place. Nobody knows what happened to him.

Dam Receives a Phone Call

Dam was busy on the roof of his house one day when the phone rang.

Quick as a flash he slid down the roof, gripped the gutter and flung himself in through a window. He landed on his feet and charged off through the door down a small corridor then through another door which he opened too quickly and accidentally banged himself on the nose. He lifted up the telephone receiver holding his nose and said in a nasal tone,

"Hello."

"Mr Diligent?" It was a woman's voice.

"Yes," said Dam.

"I'm ringing on behalf of a company which can help you with mortgage repayments." Dam felt his pockets, he hadn't any money to give her, all he had was a few roofing screws but then he thought he didn't need any more gauges anyway.

"And?" said Dam, beginning to blow his nose.

"My name is Anne" said the woman.

"And what?" asked Dam.

"Yes that's right. How did you know?"

"Eh?" said Dam.

"My name is Anne Twot" she said.

91

"I don't need any more gauges." Dam said and added, "I've got screws in my pockets at the moment and I've come off the roof." He blew his nose in the phone.

The woman laughed and asked Dam if he owned his own home.

"Oh my nose" is all he said.

"Well if you're renting we can help you."

"Renting? No it's not broken," he said.

"Are you paying it off?"

"Paying my nose off?" said Dam, who then asked, "Paying what off? I've just come off the roof, my nose is not renting and I'm screwing the roof down!"

"I see" said the lady, "and you don't own it?"

"Own what, my nose or the roof?" He asked. Then said, "Well I guess nobody owns anything really do they? Though I suppose the roof sort of owns me. I built it and I've got some of its screws in my pocket." There was a brief silence on the other end of the phone. Then Dam said,

"Anne Twot is a nice name. Tell you what," said Dam as his eyes lit up, "if you could get some more screws and come over here and help me screw the rent in my roof, I'll buy some more gauges off you if that's what you'd like and by that time my nose might feel a little better!" he snorted and the lady hung up.

Dam blew his nose again and climbed back onto the roof. As soon as he commenced work the telephone rang. Dam slid down the roof grabbed the gutter and flung himself into the room. When he picked up the phone he found another woman on the end.

"Mr Diligent?"

"Yes" said Dam cautiously.

"I wonder if you'd be interested to help with the Life Saving Appeal by buying a few tickets at $2.00 each?"

"Is that you Anne?" he said.

"No, it's Amy"

"Amy Twot?"

"No, Amy Ling."

"Oh hello" said Dam, "I was just talking to Anne Twot. Do you know her?"

"I may," said Amy.

"Yes I thought you might" said Dam.

"Can you ask her to buy me some more screws?"

"What?" said Amy.

"To help me screw on the roof!" said Dam.

"I'm running out of them and she said she'd help and come over and check me with some more gauges," he added. Then continued, "If you'd like to come over too I could save your life I'm sure. The thing is with life, you have to let it take you along Anne Twot de ya nose Amy Ling could appen!"

Amy hung up and Dam climbed back onto his roof.

Dam and the Jetty

Dam's dam had many surprises. It had hidden Dam's lawn mower after it had slipped out of his hands and driven itself into the water, it had grown ducks, tortoises, voracious weeds, and huge fish. Now the thought of catching a crocodile in it or a giant fish appealed to his imagination for often he had seen huge ripples and splashes on the surface which were obviously made by some very large creature.

He set about making many little biscuits which he thought would be good bait for whatever was in there. He ate many of them himself.

Late one evening Dam picked up his fishing rod and bait and walked out on the rickety old boards of his old jetty which he had made some years before.

At the end of it he peered into the deep dark water. It was cold and muddy, whatever it was had stirred up the bottom. The jetty wobbled a little so he sat down quietly. Taking a biscuit from his pocket he put it on his line and ate another. He lowered his line gently into the water.

Dam looked out across the dam. There were water-lilies on the far bank and here and there trees hung low to the water as though they were asleep. A frog gave a croak, the sky was clear, it would be a cool night so the snakes would not be active. Dam knew there were lots of snakes around the dam as he'd come down at night with a torch and seen many. They were attracted by all the frogs.

At that moment - as if by a sixth sense, he turned around and looked behind him. And sure enough, as Dam often sensed trouble, there on the jetty was an enormous snake! It was coming straight towards him. He leapt to his feet and the wobbly old jetty lurched sideways. He steadied himself and the snake did the same. Dam banged his foot on the jetty and yelled,

"Go away snake!" and the snake stopped and stuck out its tongue.

"The bait!" thought Dam "it can smell the bait!" He took a biscuit out of his pocket and threw it at the snake, but it missed and landed in the water.

The snake came closer and he threw another biscuit and another. The snake was even closer and Dam began to stand on one leg and then the other. He grabbed his fishing rod and tried to push the snake over the side but then one of the bits of old wood broke and he fell in the water!

Dam touched bottom it was muddy and slimy, no it wasn't the bottom, for it quickly moved away! The water was freezing and he was very frightened.

Then lots of biscuits bobbed up in the water around him. Dam looked up and saw a small splash in front of him as the snake dropped into the water and disappeared! Suddenly two huge jaws with horribly large teeth thrashed up out of the water and swallowed the snake!

"A crocodile!" shrieked Dam who began flapping about frantically trying to swim with his fishing rod. He was stuck, the water weeds were stopping him from swimming properly! At last his feet felt the muddy bottom and he began to run and swim at the same time. Finally he came to the shore puffing and panting and raced up onto the bank. He was covered in mud and weed.

He stopped and turned around to look at the dam. Everything was quiet, no sound at all! He still had his fishing rod in one hand so he began to wind in the line. To his surprise he had caught something. He pulled back hard to set the hook and at the same time something grabbed him from behind. He was pulled forward by a powerful force and sudden pain!

Dam cried out and leapt up in the air. The sudden pain made him throw his rod aside and cry out again as he tried to run further up the bank but the crocodile was holding him back!

When he settled down a little and had a closer look he found he had hooked himself really badly in the bottom.

Dam Meets a Dragon

It was one of those calm sunny winter mornings when a heavy due sparkles on the ground and wets one's feet as though walking in a shallow pool.

Dam woke early full of energy since he'd had a good meal the night before.

He sprang out of bed like a wind-up doll and decided to go for a walk on the beach. After a small breakfast of two eggs, muesli, three oranges, two bananas and ten pieces of toast he scrubbed his "bristling fangs" as he called them and drove in his little blue amphibious car down to the sandy beach. The water was bitter cold as it swamped his hairy ankles. A dog and its owner passed him and then another for this was an area where people exercised their dogs.

Dam could talk in dog language and since he was feeling a little mischievous he gave an inaudible high pitched squeal and watched as the dogs took off over the sand dunes at full speed in pursuit of the noise, their overweight owners gasping behind, cursing the animals that they should make them run.

Dam sat down to watch the surf. It was small and quiet. The last time he surfed he ended up up a tree and the last time he owned a dog it gave him fleas and that was one of the worst experiences of Dam's life because he was such a hairy person. He had a terrible time trying to get rid of them.

Dam spread his fingers out in the golden sand. But not for long something was biting him. He looked down and saw that the sand was jumping with fleas. He sprang to his feet and ran a little way down to the water. It was no use the fleas were upon him! He quickly ran and dived in the sea clothes and all but that was no use either! He could feel them crawling all over him! He hastily walked to his car. A large brown dog came up behind him sniffing the air.

Dam recognised it. It was one of his neighbours.

"Oh" said Dam in dog language, "I may be as hairy as you…" he paused and continued "and I bet at the moment I've got more fleas." The dog looked sideways at Dam then sat down and began scratching. Dam walked on he, thought he heard the dog say that his owner had fleas too.

Dam sped home. He was twisting and squirming, the fleas were having a feast. At home he had a hot hot shower and used a very potent soap. That made him feel a little better though they were in his hair and kept running in his ears to hide.

Dam became desperate; he had an idea. Years ago he'd heard about a herbal remedy that was guaranteed to work. It was mud and garlic.

Dam raced around collecting all the garlic he could find, he found lots of onions too and mashed them all up together. Next he went outside banging his ears and began to dig up the backyard looking for mud. He filled his wheel-barrow with the mixture and sat in it. He rolled in the mixture and put his head under.

Dam wiped his eyes, he could barely see, he ran over to the hose and squirted himself in the face. His body began to feel curiously tingly. He went and sat in the sun. Just then the phone rang so Dam leapt up and charged inside leaving large garlic footprints all over the floor. It was somebody asking for money.

"Can you get rid of fleas?" called Dam.

"No," came the reply, "but I can help you get rid of your money!" Dam hung up, he hadn't any money anyway. The last time he had money was pretty bad.

It was a lot easier to get rid of than fleas though. He went and filled the bath and dived in. The bath turned black and it stank. Dam began to sing,

"If I was a flea, I'd flea away and never come back on a sunny dee." He stopped and thought, "I wonder if the earth feels as itchy as I do with people like fleas digging holes in it all the time?" He sang his little song again.

"I'd flea away on a sunny dee." He sat in the chair outside in the sun to dry and watched his left arm as fleas began to rise to the surface of the hair.

Dam said damn as each one rose. These he caught one by one. After some time he seemed to be winning. He worked out that if he scratched and itched the rest of his body and not his left arm, the fleas would run down to his left arm and settle there and if he was lucky he'd catch them.

It was no good he still had fleas. The more he itched the more he itched. "Agghh" he said to himself as he scratched all over. "I'm being eaten alive!"

He sat down again and wondered what to do. Moments later he was in his car driving to the vet.

"And how big is your dog?" asked the vet holding his nose. Dam carefully considered the question as he never told a lie and always told the truth and said,

"As big as me." The vet looked at him and snarled. Dam was buying medicine to help get rid of his fleas. He took the bottle home and read the label which read if the dog weighed a certain amount one had to give it a certain number of pills. Dam swallowed the whole lot, he was not good at numbers.

"That'll get rid of them" he said as he sat down scratching his knee.

He didn't do much that day except catch fleas. He was painting the house but found it impossible for each time he reached up to paint, a flea would bite him and paint would go everywhere.

He cut some fire wood, occasionally pausing to scratch himself like a dog.

He sniffed the air - rain, Dam could smell it a mile off. Sure enough large black clouds were filling the northern horizon. It was going to be a wet night.

As Dam finished his dinner and the fleas had theirs he went to the matchbox to look for a match to light the fire. There were quite a few matches in the box but whoever used them had put the dead matches back in the box! Dam looked around as if to find another person in the room.

"Who could have done that?" he said to himself knowing full well who it was. There was one match left. "One match," he said, "I shall have to split it to make two."

He set about splitting the match and scratching his arm at the same time. Finally, with two thin matches he tried to light one on the side of the box.

It flared up, fizzed then died, just as a role of thunder sounded in the distance. Dam said damn, "Now I have only one match." Knowing full well that he had only half a match. With great care he began to split the match again but the end broke off and fell on the floor. Now on his knees and even closer with his nose he found the little ball of pink stuff which makes a match light. Scratching his leg he put some paper next to the box and burnt his finger as he scraped the side.

Rain began to patter down on the roof and thunder roared in the distance.

The match held its flame and the paper flared up then mysteriously went out. Dam quickly knelt lower and began to blow on the sparks but there must have been moisture in the paper for it soon went out!

He sat in his chair staring in the dark at the wood in the fireplace and wondered how he could start the fire. It was a cold night. He stood up and turned the light on and was about to sit back down when there was a very loud fizzing noise and a pale blue light then an almighty clap of thunder.

Dam received such a shock he could feel all his fleas shaking.

He put his fingers in his ears and sat down. When he thought the thunder had passed he took his fingers out.

"Fizz – sizzle - Bang!" The flash of lightning was blinding and he could only see white for some time. The thunder was so loud he thought the fleas were bouncing off his ear drums! He put his hands over his ears. Suddenly pop!

Out went the electric light. Then another blinding flash, the storm was overhead.

Everything went black. Then something very strange seemed to come out of the light bulb. To Dam it looked like a bright yellow ball surrounded by a blue glow. It rolled down from the ceiling and landed on the other couch in front of the fire place. It was spinning round and around quickly or slowly Dam couldn't tell. He watched it, his mouth open in amazement.

A pale orange light filled the room and around the ball of fire little sparks danced, fizzed, popped and went out. It was luminescent. As Dam watched closely the small ball, for it was only as large as his fist, began to slow down until it seemed to completely stop. Then to Dam's utter amazement in the couch opposite him sat a pink and white spotted fiery Dragon!

Rain was pouring heavily on the roof and every now and again brilliant flashes of lightning illuminated the windows and the thunder rolled and roared.

"Hello," it said. Dam was speechless. "My name is Dulcie, I know your name already Mr Diligent."

"My... me ...my, me ... my!" said Dam.

"Oh don't mind me" said the fiery Dragon stretching her luminous green wings, "I've just had a little battle with a Black Dragon from the sky and ...er...well, I decided to come and have a rest and talk to you for a while.

You see Mr Diligent, Dragons never die."

"Oh...oh," said Dam who'd forgotten completely about his fleas. "You're a Dra..Dragon?"

"Indeed I am," said Dulcie. "I'm older than you realise Mr Diligent. My folks were born when the earth was made. We used to have such fun in those volcanoes, as you people call them. To us they were like lucky-dip rides and fun parks...we had such a good time....being blasted into the air then sucked back into the earth."

"Oh, oh," said Dam who was rubbing his eyes and tapping the side of his face to see if he was awake.

"Then when earth began to cool down we Dragons, to keep warm, stayed under the ground where it was nice and hot!"

"Nice and hot" repeated Dam who was beginning to believe what he was seeing.

"It's only in storms now," continued Dulcie the fiery Dragon "that we come out and ride the lightning up into the clouds. That's fun too....stokes up our fires...ahh...ahh...oh!" She said as she lifted her long nose in the air and wrapped her tail around her. "Oh I don't want to sneeze in here," she said, "might be dragoness, I mean dangerous, but Mr Diligent its very cold!"

As she spoke Dam could see the inside of her mouth it was red and fiery.

Her eyes were vivid green and she had long hands and sharp pointed claws.

She wrapped her green wings around her body and little puffs of steam came out of her nostrils.

"Burrr, its cold ....ahh...ahh. Oh no, I must not sneeze."

Just then there was another loud clap of thunder and a brilliant flash of lightning. Rain began to thunder down on the roof.

"Oh, I had a fire going," said Dam standing up and bending over to see if there were any sparks left, "but I ran out of matches."

At that moment there was a loud "Ahrr..chew!" from the fiery Dragon and Dam was blasted into the chimney by a huge burst of flame!

"Arrgah" he yelled as he was surrounded by fire! All he could see was fire in the room. He was alight and burning fiercely! He thought the house had been hit by lightning!

"Quickly, quickly, outside in the rain!" cried Dulcie.

Dam raced to the door and flung himself into the storm. He soon went out. Miraculously he wasn't burned at all! When he came back inside he couldn't find the Dragon anywhere. He looked at his arms and legs they were black.

All his hair had been singed. His clothes had been burnt to rags however best of all there were no fleas!

He fetched a towel and dried himself and came back to stand in front of the fire which was happily burning. He looked down at the couch where the Dragon had been and stood with his back to the fire.

"Now where did she go?" he thought.

The storm was passing and Dam was thinking that the vet would not believe him when he told him that a Dragon has singed all the fleas off his dog.

"Mr Diligent, it's rude to turn your back on guests." Dam jumped and looked at the fire. Dulcie was sitting on a burning log with her legs crossed.

"Oh," said Dam "I didn't see you in there!"

"That's alright" said the little Dragon, "I'm so sorry I burnt you."

"Oh" said Dam, "I'm grateful, you got rid of all my flee…hair," he quickly said.

Dulcie laughed and puffs of flame came out of her nostrils.

"You live in a nice little house Mr Diligent…I hope you've got lots of firewood?"

"Oh," said Dam knowing that he hadn't any at all and didn't like the thought of going out again in the rain to find more.

"If I get cold...I sneeze," she said.

"I'll get some more," he said as he picked up his hat and coat and went outside to fetch wood. Presently he came back with a huge stack and set it down in front of the fire to dry.

"That will last awhile" he said.

Dulcie then asked Dam all sorts of funny questions. Whether he had a computer, a radio or a mobile phone or a micro-wave oven. Dam being poor only had what he needed and that was a radio. Dulcie seemed to know that already.

Then it was Dam's turn to ask questions and the first question he asked was where did Dragons live? Dulcie yawned as if she had been asked that before and said,

"We live in the deep earth and come out in electrical storms. Some Dragons called Black Dragons live in computers and radios and mobile phones and other things like that" she said. They can get into micro-wave ovens and cause mischief" she added.

"Black Dragons can be nasty; they try to trick us all the time. When the earth was growing a long time ago, all Dragons like me roamed around freely.

Then the continents of the earth began to move together and create a lot of electricity. Black Dragons used to ride down lightning flashes and they lived mainly in the clouds. But Dragons like me liked the earth so we stayed underground where its nice and warm. Black Dragons are always cold and always try to get inside the earth and invade our homes."

"That is why we fight with them, to keep them away. They're jealous of our warmth; we don't let them come underground. Ever since the earth closed up they have been flying around in the sky. We've been fighting with them for millions of years."

Dam put another log on the fire making sure to place it at Dulcie's feet so she was more comfortable. The fire popped and sparkled so much Dam couldn't work out which was fire and which was Dulcie. Occasionally he caught glimpses of her large green eyes watching him from within the flames.

The storm had passed though it was still raining. Dam and Dulcie stayed up all night talking about the world. Dulcie's talk always came back to the Black Dragons she seemed to think about them a lot.

Finally in the small hours of the morning the fire wood ran out and only coals remained. Dulcie made a small nest amongst them and said she was going to have a quick little sleep.

Before she closed her eyes she asked Dam if he had any batteries and could he place them on the couch. Dam had some torch batteries so he put them on the chair. He crawled into bed himself and was soon fast asleep.

Dam had a dream that he was in the sky flying along with a great flock of pink and white spotted Dragons. Suddenly from a large black cloud ahead a bolt of lightning shot out and riding down it came an army of Black Dragons all screaming and wielding small flashes of lightning as swords. There was a cry from beside him and looking he saw Dulcie the Dragon breathing fire!

Dam woke up. He was a pacifist. He went into the bathroom and found to his amazement that there was a whole lot of foul smelling black mud in the bath!

He looked up expecting to see a hole in the roof. He had forgotten that he'd put the garlic-mud there the day before.

He showered and filled the drain plug up with charcoal from all his burnt hair. He scrubbed his arms and legs and for the first time in many years he could actually see his skin!

He went into the lounge room and looked in the fireplace. Dulcie the Dragon wasn't there only a small depression in the ashes where she'd been asleep.

"Hello," came a familiar voice. Dam looked around and saw the little fiery Dragon sitting on the batteries with her long tail stuck in a power point.

"Batteries keep me warm," she said, "but Black Dragons are in the power supply of your house that's why the electricity isn't working."

"Did you sleep well?" asked Dam.

"Oh" said Dulcie, "Dragons only sleep for a few minutes." Dam asked her if she wanted some breakfast.

"Oh no" she said "We don't eat either, I'm just waiting for some more power to liven me up, thanks."

"We'd better go shopping" said Dam "I'll buy some more batteries, some candles, a new light globe and some matches…though with you around Dulcie" and he laughed, "I suppose I don't need matches." Dulcie laughed too.

After Dam had finished his usual small breakfast they went out to the car together.

"I'll ride on the battery," said Dulcie.

"The battery!" exclaimed Dam.

"Ahh.. ahh…oh," said the Dragon, "I mustn't sneeze…I need to keep warm."

Dam lifted up the bonnet of his car and Dulcie flew up onto the battery.

She stretched her wings out to touch the positive and negative terminals and a small spark danced about her.

Dam drove to the supermarket and for the first time in his life he had green traffic lights all the way.

"Did you change the lights to green?" he asked as he lifted up the bonnet of the car.

"Of course," she said as she sprang up off the battery and flew onto his shoulder.

Dam wondered what the people would think when they saw the little fiery Dragon but they didn't seem to even notice. She must have been invisible to them.

Dam pulled out a shopping trolley and went off down the isles in search of candles, batteries, a new light bulb and matches, but Dulcie seemed to know exactly where everything was.

When they were buying candles a customer's mobile phone rang.

Dulcie passed close by and seemed to be listening. The lady with the mobile was having difficulty with reception, she kept saying,

"Hello, Hello, Hello." Dulcie flew onto her shoulder and much to Dam's horror disappeared into her mobile phone!

"Dulcie!" exclaimed Dam out loud. The woman looked sideways at him and kept talking. Reception had improved. Dulcie flew back out of the phone and sat on the front of the shopping trolley.

"Those Black Dragons again," was all she said.

At the checkout Dam put his few items on the counter but as they were being counted the computer crashed and a strange noise came from it.

The checkout girl said,

"Oh no, not again" and Dulcie dived into the computer! Lots of smoke came out of the back of it then she emerged looking troubled.

"Nasty, cold Black Dragons," she said as the computer suddenly began to work again.

"Oh Mr Diligent I'm getting cold!" she said as Dam hastily opened the bonnet of the car. As he drove home through green light after green light he began to think how lucky he was to have met a real Dragon. But then he came upon a red traffic light and he stared at it then wondered if Dulcie was alright. "Ahh…ahh…ahh..chew!"

Bang! the bonnet of Dam's car blew up and flames roared into the sky.

Dam leapt out calling,

"Dulcie, Dulcie, are you alright!?" He was fanning the flames and trying to stick his head in the fire to see. Onlookers thought he'd gone mad!

"My Dragon's in there!" he kept saying. Dam could only stand back and watch as his car caught fire. Fortunately a passing motorist jumped out of another car with a fire extinguisher and put out the flames. Dam looked under his car and inside where the motor was, calling,

"Dulcie, Dulcie!" People thought he was talking to the car!

Dam walked a little way back down the road to see if she'd fallen out and been squashed but there was no sign of her.

"Oh Dulcie, Dulcie!" he cried, but then he remembered her words,

"Dragons never die!"

Dam walked home. On his way a large dog come out of a house to talk to him. Dam recognised it from the beach.

"How are your fleas?" asked the dog.

"Dulcie the Dragon got rid of them for me" Dam said.

"Is that your owner?" asked the dog. Dam did not answer, he was thinking,

"A real Dragon!"

"My owner was hit by lightning" said the dog, "it got rid of him and the fleas!"

That night it rained and another electrical storm came overhead.

As the thunder roared and the lightning flashed Dam looked up at the new electric light bulb half expecting a Dragon to pop out of it.

He lit a little fire and watched the dancing flames and for a small moment he thought he saw a little pink and white spotted Dragon with big green eyes staring back out of the flames watching him.

Dam and the Dishwasher

The first machine smashed all the plates. The cutlery was the only thing which eventually shut the machine down, luckily it became jammed.

The swaying of the machine made holes in the floor and when the fan belts blew the engine kept running until it seized and went red hot and nearly burnt the house down.

The second machine was a little more gentle though Dam somehow managed to get stuck inside it. He had to lick all the greasy plates he was in there for so long. Miraculously one day the door flew open and he escaped. His plates were unbelievably clean! He thought he might get a job as a dishwasher and eat a lot of soap before starting.

This second machine was quite effective. One day he opened it up before it had stopped and a fork flew out at him. He quickly shut the door and removed the fork from his top pocket where it had conveniently landed.

This machine was quite a marvel considering that it was made out of an old car. Dam could put his washing in it and at times even sat in there himself fully clothed to get clean though it was a little cramped as the blade of the rotor passed just under his nose. Dam's top lip was very clean.

The noise of the thing was annoying however so Dam packed all around the outside of it with cardboard and then cement. He used to sit in there with ear-muffs on until one time the rotor-arm became entangled in the muffs and he nearly lost his life.

For some strange reason he liked to sit inside and watch everything going around and around. With various pipes sticking out of it at all angles and the four wheel-hubs of the car clearly visible he would set it in motion. It worked beautifully and only slightly hummed.

After sometime Dam noticed a crack in the floor then another and another and it wasn't long before the dishwasher began to sink into the floor! Dam crawled under his house to have a look and sure enough the thing was pushing the foundations under as well! Even as he watched there was a loud groaning noise and the dishwasher descended a little more.

It wasn't long before he had to step down to open the door of it. Then late one night there was a loud groaning and crunching noise from the kitchen.

Dam raced out just in time to see his machine disappearing into the earth and even as he watched the soil about it fell back into place until there was no sign that anything was ever there!

Dam woke up. Had he dreamt it? He went out to the dishwasher and no, there was the huge hole in the floor alright. The pipes had been pulled out of the wall and he could hear a faint humming sound. He didn't know what to do.

He simply cut all the pipes and left it there. Even when he turned the electricity off to it he could still hear it humming far beneath the house!

Would he make another dishwasher and risk putting another hole in his house? Dam ate finger-food for months after that and to this day he still hasn't built another machine.

Dam and the Possum

Dam liked bananas. If there was one fruit he really liked it was bananas.

One day he was out driving, eating a banana when he came around a corner and found two ladies trying to drag a fallen log off the road.

"Silly bananas," he said to himself.

"A second earlier and it would have smashed our car!" they said as they struggled to move it. Dam got out and put his weight behind the log but it would not move. The ladies came over to his side and all three pushed and strained and soon there was just enough room for one car to pass.

Huffing and puffing Dam said,

"You go!"

"But what about you?" they cried "you can't hold this!" But little did they know they were talking to Dam Diligent.

"Go!" huffed Dam. The ladies quickly got in their car and drove around the tree. Dam's grip began to slip. His shoes began to role on the small stones and in an instant he was catapulted back the other side of the road where he fell in a ditch.

Dam fetched some rope and tied it to the tree and tied the other end to the rear axle of his car. He drove slowly in the direction of the ditch and the tree began to bend again. It bent as though it would never break. His wheels were close to the ditch when suddenly with a loud snap the tree broke in half.

Dam's car sped nose first into the ditch.

When he was untying his rope a little pink nose and two funny ears popped up out of a hole in the tree.

"Oh what do we have here?" said Dam as he put his hands in and pulled out a tiny baby possum. It looked at him with huge black eyes and didn't struggle at all. Dam took it back to the car and put it on the back seat and wrapped it in a jumper. He then went back to the tree to look for the mother but try as he might he couldn't find her.

"I will have to take you home little Tarzan," he said.

Soon another car came along and was able to tow Dam's car out of the ditch. Dam looked in the back and saw that Tarzan was asleep. But not for long for as soon as Dam began to eat a banana Tarzan climbed onto the seat next to his shoulder and sniffed in his ear and then tried to reach out and grab the fruit. Dam drove home with Tarzan eating a banana on his shoulder.

There was one fruit Tarzan liked and that was bananas. Tarzan could not get enough of them. He was growing fat. Dam had a banana patch out the back and at times produced an excess of the fruit. He had tried drying them and freezing them. Quite often he and Tarzan would fight over a banana. Dam would always win but he'd give Tarzan a little piece. Tarzan became fanatical and even ate green bananas! Dam didn't like that at all because he was trying to make green banana wine.

He had a large bottle which he kept in the kitchen and into this bottle he put two whole bunches of bananas and lots of brown sugar. It hissed and popped for weeks. Tarzan thought Dam was stupid the way he used to look at it. In fact Tarzan thought Dam was a little simple the way he used to watch himself in the mirror. Tarzan already knew what Tarzan looked like and didn't bother with the mirror at all.

Dam and Tarzan got along quite well until Dam decided to give Tarzan his first bath as he was smelly. Poor possum did not like it! So Dam settled him down with some green banana wine. Tarzan sat in the bath at one end sipping his banana wine and Dam sat up the other end whistling and singing to himself with the soap.

Dam tried to learn possum language and he found he could communicate better after he'd drunk some green banana wine. He used to play hide and seek with Tarzan and Tarzan would squeal with excitement. Sometimes Dam would run around the table on all fours yabbering in possum language. Tarzan couldn't understand a word, though he did understand how Dam felt when Dam hit his head on the table.

Best of all Tarzan liked looking at picture books while sitting up in Dam's bed! And since it was a cold winter Tarzan used to sleep at Dam's feet at night to keep each other warm. Tarzan snored, it took Dam sometime to get used to the noise.

Tarzan grew bigger and bigger. His tail was as long as Dam's leg. He'd scare Dam sometimes by jumping on his shoulder from the table. Tarzan was too large for games like that. He was even getting too big for Dam's bed! Sometimes Dam would wake up on the floor having been pushed out of bed by the great big black possum. Dam loved Tarzan though and he was never angry at him.

Until one day Dam returned home from shopping to find an incredible mess in the house. Then Tarzan lunged at him and grabbed him round the head from behind. Dam couldn't see. Eventually he untied himself from Tarzan and saw the mess. Green banana wine everywhere and one drunken possum. Tarzan was uncontrollable he was leaping about the room and hanging from the light in the middle of the ceiling by his tail.

"Out! Out" shrieked Dam. "Outside and stay out!" he said thinking possums are for the outdoors anyway. Tarzan did a backflip down the stairs and chased Dam around the table then ran outside and chased his tail around on the lawn.

Dam shut the door and went inside. He spent hours mopping and cleaning up the mess. Tarzan had hidden all Dam's knives and forks. Some were behind pictures on the walls and he found some forks above the door. The telephone had been pulled out of the wall and thrown in the sink. Worse than that the floor was covered in green banana wine and the mirror had disappeared!

"That is the last time Tarzan is coming in here!" Dam said as he eventually lay his head on the pillow but he soon sat up. Tarzan had put the mirror under Dam's pillow and it was cracked!

"Tarzan will have to sleep up trees where he belongs."

At about three o'clock that morning Dam was rudely awakened by Tarzan jumping on the roof. Since Dam had a tin roof the noise was deafening.

Bang, crash, bang! Dam was wide awake in seconds.

"Be quiet Tarzan" he yelled. Tarzan stopped then bang, bang, bang and ran, clatter, clatter, clatter, till he was just above Dam's bed. Then bang, bang, bang, until he leapt off into a tree. Dam snuggled back down but it was no use he was wide awake. Tarzan did not appear the next day.

"Probably dropped dead from too much wine, ashamed to show his face!" thought Dam.

That night when Dam was having dinner he looked across at Tarzan's empty chair and thought how wonderful and peaceful it was too eat dinner alone.

He went to bed early because he hadn't slept well the night before.

Bang, bang crash, crash – again!

"Tarzan be quiet!" yelled Dam. It was two o'clock in the morning. Tarzan had boots on. He was walking flat-footed and bouncing up and down.

Dam hid under the sheets.

"Oh go away" he moaned. Dam slept in. At ten o'clock he staggered out of bed and slumped into a chair.

"Possum!" is all he could say. The same thing happened the next night and the next. Tarzan was growing bigger and making more noise! He seemed to know the right moment when Dam was snoring or in his deepest sleep.

Bang! Bang! Bang! rattle, rattle, rattle, Tarzan was back.

"I can't go on!" said Dam looking in the broken mirror. "I'll have to get rid of him. Catch him or something and let him go fifty kilometres away."

He went outside to pick some bananas and it was then he realised why Tarzan was jumping on the roof. He was feeding on all Dam's banana plants and there was only one bunch left, Tarzan had eaten all the rest!

"That does it," said Dam. "I'll have to make a trap!"

He cut the last bunch down and took them inside. "Tarzan isn't going to get these" he said.

Tarzan didn't get them, the banana wine did! Dam pushed them into his brewing bottle and watched the bubbles rise.

Dam staggered about, he hadn't had any sleep for days. He drank some wine and went to bed early. Bang! Bang, on the roof. Dam raced outside in the dark in his pyjamas with a torch and just saw Tarzan leap off the roof into the guava tree. He climbed to the top of the tree and began to eat a guava and peered down at Dam and began to laugh. Dam stormed back inside, he was devising a trap in his mind.

The next day Dam went to his shed and found some old fish net and some strong rope. He tied one piece of the rope to the tallest branch of the guava tree and the other end of it to the net. He then pulled the tree down as hard as he could and with a smaller piece of rope tied to a trigger-stick, he set the trap.

He spread the net around the trigger-stick and baited it with his last bottle of green banana wine.

That night Dam slept right through. Tarzan did not wake him. Dam woke in the morning thinking he'd caught him and ran outside. The trap had not gone off. Tarzan was not interested in the guavas or the bottle of green banana wine. And there weren't any bananas left.

"He'll be back" said Dam. But Tarzan didn't come back. Dam waited a week and still no Tarzan. He even woke up at all hours in the early morning expecting to hear a crash on the roof. No sound, only quiet. Tarzan had gone away.

He lay back down and was thinking about his possum, what a rascal he was!

It was nearly dawn before he finally went to sleep.

One evening it was hot and Dam couldn't sleep. He woke up early in the morning thinking Tarzan was on the roof but he wasn't. Dam couldn't get back to sleep, he was thirsty. Without thinking he took his torch and went looking for his last bottle of green banana wine.

Whoomp! Up in the air went Dam, the torch went one way and Dam went the other still clutching his bottle of green banana wine.

"Damn!" said Dam as he bounced up and down in the net. He struggled a little making sure not to drop his bottle. He felt like an insect in a spider's web. After a while he stopped struggling and lay back to look at the stars. He was cold at last and shivered. He opened the bottle, prizing the metal top off with his teeth.

There in the net, four feet above the ground while he gently swayed, he sipped his wine and finally fell asleep and unbeknown to him his snoring could be heard for miles.

The early morning found him suspended in his trap. He complimented himself on the efficiency of it, though wished he was sitting at the kitchen table eating breakfast.

Over the next few days Dam had plenty of time to think and catch up on lost sleep. Nobody came to rescue him. He began to wonder if anybody would! Eventually he realised that he might be there until he died if he didn't do something about it.

He reached through the net and tried to tear some leaves off the guava tree to eat. He managed to reach two. He felt a bit like a possum as he sat in the net and chewed them.

He was starving, he hadn't eaten for days! He took the top off the bottle and began to cut through the net. If only he could smash the bottle he thought - hit it on something hard then he could use the glass to cut the net. The only thing hard was his head and after a few blows he felt rather sore and gave up.

He hit his knee but that was worse. Now his knee and head ached!

All day he worked at the net with the bottle-top until finally he cut through one strand.

"At last!" he said to himself. Dam was desperate; he worked deep into the night sawing away at another strand. He couldn't undo the knots they were too tight then late in the night he dropped the bottle top. He could just see it like a little star twinkling on the ground.

Early the next day he began to jump up and down like Tarzan in the hope that his weight would bring him down close enough to the bottle-top for him to reach out and grab it. But it was no use. At lunch time he gave up and sat in the net glaring at the new banana bunches which were forming.

Late that night Dam was awakened by movement in the tree. He was swaying gently and seemed to be going down. Looking up he could just make out a huge black shape above him in the tree. It was Tarzan, he'd come back!

Dam watched him carefully as he didn't want to frighten him. Dam noticed he looked terribly thin. Tarzan looked down at Dam and in possum language said hello. Dam said hello back. Tarzan wasn't interested in Dam, all he wanted was a guava at the top of the tree. Dam looked down at the bottle-top. Tarzan's weight was bringing him closer and closer to it. Until he reached out and snatched it up just as Tarzan took the guava.

He held the fruit in his little claws and climbed back down the tree. He came along the ground and handed the guava up to Dam who had tears in his eyes for Tarzan was very thin. Dam handed half the guava back and ate one half.

It was very bitter but he ate it all and chewed it very well. Tarzan sat up and ate his half and looked at Dam.

The next day Dam cut another thread through and the following day another. Till at long last he slid out of the hole in the net and fell onto the ground.

He was very thin too, though now he was free. He stumbled into his house and drank some water and had a small meal. Tarzan had saved his life.

That night Dam put some old crusts of bread on the roof of his house. Tarzan came and ate them. Dam slept soundly and in the morning emptied his large bottle of green banana wine down the sink. The thought of drinking more made him feel sick.

Several days later he cut a bunch of bananas and left some of them on the roof. Very early in the morning before dawn Dam heard Tarzan walking quietly on the roof, sit down and eat the bananas. Dam went back to sleep.

The next night there was a little tap on the door. Dam opened it and found Tarzan on the doorstep looking very thin. He let him come inside and gave him some bread and more bananas. Tarzan sat on Dam's knee and talked the whole time. When Tarzan had finished he curled up on Dam's lap and went to sleep.

"Oh no!" said Dam "not there." And with that he took Tarzan the great big black smelly possum and put him at the foot of his bed, climbed in to bed himself and soon they were both snoring.

Dam Creates a Magnetic Field

Dam was used to eating iron filings for breakfast, he didn't have any teeth either, he'd lost them in a kick-boxing bout with a woman. Dam was ready for anything now. The extra iron in his diet would make him strong in heart and body. He could for instance eat whole brake-cylinders. He would wash them down with strong tea muttering how they would stop anything.

Dam made his own iron filings, he found bits and pieces of iron to use from everywhere. He felt like a good car, strong and heavy. It was true Dam had an attraction to metal especially when he swallowed a magnet. He had found a giant magnet from a large loud-speaker and had some of it for breakfast the next day and the next. In fact it was so large it took him a week to eat! He became so magnetised. He decided he would never lose his car keys again as he could stick them anywhere on his body. He could make doors fly open if he went into kitchens. Fridges and dishwasher doors would open in greeting and if Dam wasn't careful all the knives and forks would fly up and attach to him. Once he became glued to a revolving door and had to go backwards and forwards for a long time. It took six men to pull him off!

One day he was crossing a bridge and trying to avoid the pull of each car as it passed when he lost his balance, fell off and landed in the water. A fellow in a boat saw him hit the water and threw him a rope which Dam managed to grab, but he sank! Dam was a good swimmer normally. The boat went to shore and many people came down to the water and began pulling on the rope.

Dam must have become stuck and after some time an amazing sight met their eyes for out of the water came an unidentified sea creature never before seen with bits of metal sticking out of him all over the place! It was then Dam decided to start a scrap metal yard, where he could be used on the end of a crane to dredge rivers and lakes for metal.

Dam entertained his rescuers with a story about a woman who lived in the hills who had at least three horses which could look in her bedroom window but alas she didn't have any shoes for them to wear.

"This lady," continued Dam, "was just about to go to sleep when there was a knock on the door and there on the doorstep was a scrap-iron merchant with fourteen horse shoes on him. He had twelve in his hands and was actually standing on two!" The small crowd stood there listening as he pulled the last fish-hook from his hair.

One of the rescuers found an old clock and another found a kettle, some small tins full of mud lots and lots of fish hooks, a few pots and a whole lot of wire. Dam had two bicycle frames and three car hubcaps attached as well.

"And do you know what she said to him?" Dam continued. But they were walking away shaking their heads and murmuring something about a "magnetic personality." Dam was left there cold and wet surrounded by a junk yard.

He delicately tip-toed through but jumped when he saw a large bail of wire moving toward him and unfortunately he began to collect all sorts of other things on his left foot! He fell over. The wire came rolling towards him and with it several other pieces of junk. The wire stuck to him and suspended him in the air as more junk flew up to meet him.

He stayed there for a full high tide. Not many people could see him due to the amount of metal attached. The water came up and touched his toes.

Night was coming on and he was face down, he could barely move. At some time in the night he heard the sound of an approaching boat.

"At last!" he thought he would be rescued. The tide was up and the boat drew awfully close.

"Bang!" Dam was wrenched aside and jammed onto the side of the boat.

"Here get a light on this!" cried a startled man leaning overboard. Soon a light came on and shone into Dam's eyes.

"That's the weirdest looking sea creature I've ever seen!" said the man.

With great difficulty they hauled him aboard and studied the strange wreckage. Peering through the metal they caught Dam's eyes and in a mumbled voice Dam said.

"I'm a magnetised man."

"Cripes!" came the reply, "You're not going to blow up are you?"

Dam Develops a Limp

Dam's table manners were appalling. His beard was so long he quite often got it entangled in his food and more than once he'd fished unchewed mouthfuls from his stomach which had become attached to his beard.

He hated using forks because they were always dirty in between the prongs and if he missed his mouth... well a fork could blind you. Dam ate with a spoon always, he'd sharpened one edge of it. He had a fishing knife which he used to cut up the vegetables with. Yes Dam ate vegetables that was why he'd reached such a healthy old age. One hundred and twenty. He looked in the mirror and belched.

Often his beard stuck out at odd angles and sprouted from unmentionable places, why it was even coming out of his ears! The first time he smoked a cigar somebody offered him and kindly lit, his nose exploded in a forest fire and he couldn't get used to the burnt flesh smell for weeks.

Dam was sick of cutting his own hair there wasn't any above his forehead.

It wasn't old age which made him bald it was actually a golfing accident.

"I'll go and get a proper hair cut in town" he said to himself in the mirror, "and I'll walk."

He set off early one morning, it was only six hours to town. He took a few short cuts and came upon some curb and guttered road three kilometres out. One of Dam's hobbies was collecting scrap metal, bits of brass and copper and often he found this in the gutter. He proceeded to walk one foot in the gutter and one foot on the top of it, so he was going up and down. From a distance he looked like he had a limp.

By the time he reached the barbers he swore one leg was shorter than the other. Even on flat ground he couldn't stop going up and down. Dam said,

"Damn! I've developed a limp!"

He hobbled into the barber's and sat down. He had found some brass screws and a large odd shaped piece of copper. These things spiked him a bit through his pants.

Soon it was his turn and he limped up to the chair. The barber gripped him by the shoulders and flung him back in the chair and then made the chairs' legs fly up in the air. Dam watched as his legs flew up in the air too.

The brass screws fell out of Dam's pockets and sprinkled on the floor. He felt trapped, unable to pick them up. The barber was lashing him with some foul smelling white powder.

The barber leant forward and exhaled and Dam realised he'd been holding his breath.

"Do you ever wash?" he said to Dam who showed his yellow teeth and stuck his green tongue out.

"Just make me look nice," he scoffed.

When the barber had finished he threw the scissors away. There was hair all over the floor. Dam looked at himself in the mirror as the chair bounced back up. He sat there staring for quite some time. It was a complete stranger who met his eyes.

"A bit of a toupee on the bald patch and you'd pass for a youngster" said the barber brushing Dam's shoulders again.

"What's a toupee?" inquired Dam.

"Toupee or not toupee" said the barber and showed Dam a slab of skin with some hair on it and placed it delicately on Dam's forehead.

"Oh I like that" said Dam.

"You glue it on with this" said the barber handing Dam a little brown bottle. Dam was so impressed he bought the toupee and the glue and completely forgot about the brass screws he'd left on the floor.

He thanked the barber and went outside with his toupee still on his head, he'd stuck it on with a little bit of saliva. Fortunately his limp had disappeared.

As he was walking down the main street he noticed a small sign which read "Dancing Lessons."

Now thought Dam is the time to be a little more correct, well-mannered and nice, perhaps dancing will help my social life he thought. He went inside.

There were several people dancing, ladies in long dresses and men looking like penguins. "Oh tut, tut," said Dam to himself, "this is the place for me!"

Just then an elderly lady came up to the front desk mumbling something about a dinner party and that she needed one more guest to come.

"How do you do?" said Dam in his most gracious manner bowing slightly.

"Oh!" said the lady.

"And I doo like your dress!" said Dam.

"You do?" said the lady taken aback.

"Yes," said Dam and added "most charming." The lady's eyes lit up like candle sticks and Dam flared his newly revealed nostrils. This was one of Dam's unfortunate traits, some throwback gene akin to dog sniffing, the lady curiously watched them go out and in.

"I haven't a clue how to dance" he continued, "I suppose you know how to be effortless and lithe?" he inquired. Dam was biting his tongue; awkward thing it quite often got in his way!

"Oh I am in such a hurry" said the lady. "But please Mr...err" "Diligent," said Dam rather quickly.

"Would you like to come to my dinner party tonight?"

"Oh!" said Dam, "I'd be delighted!" and added "I'm in a dreadful hurry myself, may I be of assistance?"

"Oh" said the lady, "I have to wait for my chauffer outside."

"May I?" said Dam offering his arm

"Oh" she squeaked. As they went back out onto the footpath Dam found he'd developed his limp again. "Damn," he said to himself under his breath.

"Oh" she said, "you've got a limp?"

"Arrgh!" said Dam.

"You poor man. Can I give your lift a limp somewhere?" then realising her tangle of words and batting her eyelids she said, "Can I give your limp a lift?"

"Oh!" said Dam, "thank you." Dam swung his large lump of copper in between them as they sat in the car on the back seat together.

She looked down at him and said,

"Are you feeling alright?" he looked up at her and said,

"I'm so excited about coming to your party! I'm only going a little way." He said turning to her, "I feel like I've known you for years - but what is your name?" Dam squinted, she was too close to him, his eyesight wasn't too good, some things looked large and others small. He flared his nostrils but that didn't help. At the moment all he could see was a huge nose next to him.

Then he caught her eyes, sort of set in a bit, like little pools in the bottom of an open-cut mine. Dam flared his nostrils again and he grabbed his nose.

"Betty" she said showing her smile. "But you may call me Beth, or my friends call me Birth, whatever you wish," she said looking at him and flickering her eyelashes again.

Dam's hearing was not too good either and he mistook "Beth" for "Death" and "Birth" for "Dirth."

"Dirth is such a nice name" he said. And continued, "My name is Damuall"

"Ah, Damuall, that's nice too!" Now her teeth were as big as elephant's tusks sticking out in front gnashing the air.

There was silence as each person melded to the electrical impulses of the other and the lump of copper began to warm.

"Oh I'll be there!" he said as he deftly opened the door and stepped onto the pavement. He had guided the chauffer to the richest part of town and alighted as though he lived in that very street.

"Damuall, I'll see you at seven!"

"Wonderful Dirth!" he said as he closed the door gently. Their eyes met momentarily through the pain of glass before she was whisked away.

Dam went back to going up and down in the gutter. His heart was peppering along as he felt his great lump of copper warming in his pocket.

When he arrived home it was quite late. He only had time to shower and change his clothes. He cleaned his teeth with wood ash and soap. He fashioned his clothes to suit the shoes. The shoes he polished till he could see himself in them and his socks had holes in them were nearly matching. He was ready.

"Oh you do look dashing!" he said to himself in the mirror. He took out the toupee and examined the fluff. He sniffed it and imagined the poor dead person who once owned the hair and skin now all rotten and shrivelled in the ground.

Dam washed it in soap and it changed colour considerably. He looked at the glue bottle it said "Poison do not eat" on the side of it. Since the toupee was wet he decided to put it on in the car. As Dam rarely wore shoes he found them a little awkward and as he was going down the steps to his car he misjudged his footing and half fell. When he righted himself he found that his limp had returned.

"Arrgh!" he said as he rubbed his sprained foot. But then he thought he might look more his age and sophisticated if he carried a walking stick. "No" he said, "look silly."

He went back inside because he had decided to pick some flowers to take to Dirth. He fetched his fishing knife and found an old stick which he used to prop the door open with during strong winds. "Just in case" he said to himself as he closed the door and limped down the steps his little car.

Dirth's house was quite some distance away on the other side of town.

Dam drove the long way as he was looking for some roses. He found some in a park and quick as a flash drove over the gutter, drove over the grass and pulled up alongside, leaned out his window and cut them with his fishing knife and threw them in the back. He needed more. He spied some in a front garden behind a high fence. Just as he was peeping over the top of the fence with his knife between his teeth a light went on in the house and a man came out on the veranda just above the fence. He immediately saw Dam through the roses. Neither of them said a word. Dam lowered himself back down the fence and slowly limped over to his car. Two roses were all he had, well that would have to do.

Once outside Dirth's house he took out his toupee and the little bottle of glue. He put some on his finger and applied it to the back of the toupee then placed it gently on his head. The glue felt cold and tingled a little. He combed it with his fingers and eyed himself left and right.

"God you poor devil" he said thinking again of the unhairy dead man, whose hair was about to have a rebirth at a dinner party.

Dam was excited. He grabbed the roses and leapt up the steps. "Argh!" he cried as his foot reminded him of its injury. So he limped back to his car picked up the walking stick and hobbled up to the front door. He peeped inside a window and saw a formidable sight.

He gave a slight gasp. There were people exquisitely dressed in ironed pants and shirts and women in long dresses. Dam fidgeted in one of his coat pockets. Worst of all the light was so bright it hurt his eyes, for in his own home he only had candles. He began blinking uncontrollably which made his toupee wobble. The door was slightly open and he cautiously edged towards it sideways like a three legged crab, still looking through the window.

"May I take your coat?' said a stuffy looking chap at the door who looked like he'd just jumped out of a broom cupboard. Dam, startled a bit, said

"Oh no ...thank you, it's got things in it I might need." He tried to remember what was in each pocket as he walked through the door - an apple, some dried fruit, his tooth-brushes a little bag of wood ash, his fishing knife, shifting spanner, a fancy rude cigarette lighter in the shape of the male reproductive organ (this he had brought in a foreign country years before). He even had a small hacksaw, address book, three pens, three meters of tissue paper, a radio and several bits of torn up sheets to use as handkerchiefs.

Suddenly the air assailed him. Dam stopped dead in his tracks. Cigar smoke, oh no! He was allergic to tobacco. He fidgeted for the salt container in his coat pocket and sprinkled copious quantities in his mouth hoping to alley any reaction to the smoke. He held his breath and charged forth with the roses at the fore.

"Damuall Diligent, how lovely to see you!"

"Argh, D...Death." he said temporarily forgetting her name and trying not to release his salty breath.

"Oh for me?"

"Roses" he replied taking a terrific inward breath and puffing his chest out while bowing slightly, a thing he found difficult to do!

"For a sweet, with a sweet" he said flaring his nostrils.

"Ooh!" she pulled in her clothes. She was dressed in a lime green dress and red stockings which had white-lace all the way up to her neck. How she'd ever managed to get in it was a mystery. He was half thinking about how he would get it off when he forgot his sore ankle and quickly changed legs with the stick in between.

At that moment Death reached out a hand and clasped the roses and wrenched them rather quickly from Dam's hands.

"Aargh!" she said, "you prick!" as she tossed them to the other hand and watched a little bead of blood form on her finger tip. She wiped it on her dress.

"Oh so sorry" said Dam superstitiously and pulled a meter of tissue paper out of his top pocket.

"Come Damuall I'd like you to meet some of my guests."

Dam followed unaware that he was holding his breath again as he cantilevered himself towards a large doorway into a cavernous room.

There were chandeliers hanging from the ceiling and a group of musicians were playing a waltz. It was then that Dam felt relieved that he had brought his stick at least he had a good excuse not to dance, in actual fact he knew how to dance but like his table manners you had to see it to believe it! He stood there watching as several couples giddied themselves and then ungiddied themselves before him. To Dam they all looked like they could all do with some more centrifugal gearing.

Presently a butler (that's what Dam presumed he was) came and offered them a drink, it looked like orange floor polish. Death took one and handed it to Dam,

"Oh you must try this," she said pushing it under his nose. Dam opened his mouth to speak and his salty breath exhaled.

"But.." he said.

"Oh, go on…. do you no harm." Dam graciously took the glass and stretched his lips across his face and took a minute sip.

"Oh wonderfully pique" he said as his teeth burst through his lips. "A...."

"Damask" said Death butting in.

"Shimply shitting err,..." said Dam.

"Oh Henry, come here, I want you to meet a new friend of mine, Damuall ...err"

"Diligent" said Dam, sensing she'd forgotten his name already.

"Ahh Damuall!" he said like a long lost sailor, "Pleased to meet you!" he nearly broke every bone in Dam's hand as he shook it. "I'm sure Birth is looking after you!"

Death excused herself as a woman came floating towards them. Swaying like an unbalanced ancient measuring device. Dam had the distinct feeling Death was avoiding the approaching form.

"How do you do, I'm Mary," she said holding out her long slender gloved hand. Dam held it coyly in the tips of his fingers and felt the fingers beneath become warm and soft like mouldy sausages. Her face was plastered like a Van Gogh oil painting with so much powder and to Dam she appeared as though she was about to explode a veritable primed muzzle-loader and create a blizzard of washing powder. Her eyes looked like little green peas in mashed potato. As she spoke her hair skated across her forehead and rose and fell from her face, much of it covered her black dress like snow.

"This is Damuall Innocent" said Henry.

"So delighted to meet you" said Dam lifting a leg.

"Cigar?" questioned Henry. "Argh," thought Dam, so here is the drug pusher, the fumigant, the toxic war-lord! Dam frowned at him and said in a sweet voice,

"Oh I'm....." He was cut short by Mary who said,

"Ooh Henry, may I?" She rustled amongst the sticks and found a little brown one which she stuck in her wanton mouth.

"You must" she said to Dam.

"Thank you" he said as he found one also. He saw his hand automatically descend into the tin and return like some trained military personnel.

"Oh dear I've forgotten my lighter its over on the table, excuse me." Henry bounded off feeling himself all over and Mary pulled the cigar out of her face. Unfortunately half her face rubberised and pulled out with it for it stuck to her lips. The end of it was blood red. Dam noticed her lips were still adequately rouged. He said he had a lighter and proceeded to shuffle through his pockets. He found it and drew it out before her. But alas it was the wrong object and a large shifting spanner spanned the gap between them.

"Oh" said Dam, hastily putting it away.

"Here you are" said Henry returning with the lighter which was duly struck. Mary lit her cigar and Dam shifted a leg and flared his nostrils. She looked into Dam's eyes as she took her first breath. Dam watched the heavy smoke kiss and sink in between her yellow teeth. He felt himself being drawn in much like the smoke. He steadied himself. Mary smiled and looked alluringly at Dam's toupee which wiggled and tingled.

Dam directed the cigar at the lighter but was too eager and drew in the gas instead of flame thus extinguishing the lighter. Henry restruck the flame.

Dam put it out again and drew in more gas. Henry re-struck the flame but the same thing happened. He was about to do it again when Mary said,

"Oh let me do it for you" and before Dam could wince she'd taken his cigar and thrust it in her pursed lips and held Henry's lighter hand and even manipulated his thumb to strike!

"Thank goodness," thought Dam, "now I won't have to inhale the smoke." Mary handed it back to him covered in lipstick.

"Thank you" he said feeling embarrassed. He put it in his dry mouth, it felt slimy and wet.

"I don't really smoke" he went on. "In fact tobacco makes me feel quite ill."

"Oh" said Henry "you'd better be careful." He turned his head somewhat to one side as if to look for dirt behind Dam's ears and said, "Mr Innocent, may I ask you what line of business are you in?"

"Line of business?" thought Dam well err, he had never been asked that question before!

He thought a moment longer then said,

"Car manufacturing, aircraft maintenance, ship building, rocket assemblage and golf."

"Golf!" said Mary, "I love golf!"

"Oh do you?" said Dam and added, "Most dangerous game in the world." Mary squealed with delight and produced a veritable snow storm with associated cloud cover. Dam took a minute sip of his wine - God it was awful!

He was about to tell her about his golfing accident when he noticed a slight tingling sensation from his toupee. "Ouch," he said, "that's strange."

So he changed tack and said, "The agony of golf depends on how hard you hit your balls!"

Both Henry and Mary looked at Dam dry faced. Dam shifted a leg momentarily juggling his cigar to the other hand. In fact he was having great difficulty managing the stick and the wine. Fortunately the atmosphere in the room changed and Dam shifted towards a table where he could put down the glass. But something else was wrong. His toupee was tingling more and Dam's eyes-brows began to rise and fall with a painful itch which made him flare his nostrils even more. He reached up and scratched at it gaining temporary relief, but he said under his breath, that the individual whose hair it was must have had nits.

Meanwhile Henry had excused himself and moved on while Mary was edging closer into Dam's binocular vision. Her snow covered mountainous landscape looking positively Himalayan in proportion, with the prospect of an avalanche very real.

"You sound like an expert at golf," she inquired peering beyond his eyes.

"Oh?" said Dam, who had never really played, "I'm not that good?"

Mary then began asking all sorts of questions about golf and Dam avoiding her eyes was more interested to find out why his toupee was stinging so much. His forehead was wrinkled and the toupee massively mobile. Eventually he could stand it no longer and without warning dodged sideways rapidly and disappeared behind some dancers leaving Mary's hopes wrapped in a cool breeze.

With cigar in one hand and stick in the other Dam hopped down a corridor. He had to find a mirror, a toilet, anywhere to see what was wrong with his toupee. Presently he came to a cupboard and seeing no one around he opened the door and disappeared inside. It was black and smelt of cleaning agents and old clothes. He hastily reached for his toupee and tore it off. It was stuck too well though and only the hair came out. He scratched again and eventually gained a hold of it and quickly pulled.

"Argh" he yelled as it felt as painful as the old golfing injury. He felt his forehead it was stinging like crazy. He tried to find a light switch but couldn't locate one. Then he felt for his lighter which he found and managed to strike a flame. A huge bolt of fire shot into the air and remained there until he turned the gas control down. He looked at the toupee in the flame and in a sudden ball of light it caught fire and exploded. He droppedt it on the floor and as he bent down to pick it up noticed a black horse-hair broom with soft hair. He picked the broom up along with what was left of the smouldering toupee.

And proceeded to find his fishing knife. Once found he cut a neat section of hair from the broom and took his small toupee-glue bottle out and then decided that it may be poison after all so he did not use it and looked about for something else to use.

Scratching around like a giant rodent he looked on the shelves and found some black shoe polish. He smeared some of the horse hairs through it like a brush and after a little while he had something which vaguely resembled the original hair. He then smeared his forehead with boot polish and placed it gently and pressed it down firmly. Dam's fingers were black so he wiped them on some clothes which were hanging in the cupboard.

Just then the door flew open and Dam got such a shock he nearly hit the roof. Whoever it was who opened the cupboard got an enormous fright as well and slammed the door shut, then suddenly opened it again. It was Death staring him in the face.

"Good Lord Damuall, there you are, what are you doing in there?" Dam quickly extinguished the lighter and grasping his stick limped outside saying,

"This is obviously not the toilet."

"Ah you silly man" she said smiling, "you should've asked." With that she took his arm and marched him to the appropriate door. She looked down at Dam as she was a little taller than he and saw the lipstick from Dam's cigar and several smears of dark across his face, she thought they may be bruises. "Oh" she said, "I see Mary has been taking care of you!"

"Yes" said Dam, remembering her golf, "she wanted me to teach her some special strokes."

"In there," said Death pointing to a door with a ribbon on it. "And don't disappear I need a stroke too, dinner is being served."

"Thank you" said Dam most gratefully adding "toupee or not toupee" as he entered. Dam turned the corner and bumped into the metal waste paper basket which made an incredible racket!

At least the stinging had gone from his forehead. When he faced the mirror he was shocked to see that half his face was black! He plunged his hands into his pockets and produced three meters of tissue paper and tried to wipe it all off but it smeared everywhere and crossed his nose to the other side. Dam had turned suddenly very dark! He rubbed furiously as though he was avoiding some inevitable calamity. He surveyed the damage with the eye of a peacock, preening itself one side and then the other. He spat on his fingers and tamped all the loose hairs flat. He flared his nostrils as the air had suddenly changed to the smell of boot polish. Gathering his stick and still rubbing his face, he left the room and joined the throng at the dinner table.

Death had positioned him next to her and Henry sat opposite. Dam limped over to his chair and took off his coat and hung it on the back of the chair and sat down. He looked down the table where jewellery hung poised above cleavages like huge jelly-fish about to drop. Where diamonds twinkled from powdery earlobes and false teeth flashed - the envy of any Australian sheep farmer. Dam inspected the table, the white table-cloth, very different from his newspaper, the highly polished knives and forks, very different from his single spoon which was sharpened on one side.

He was about to put his arms on the table and quickly changed their direction and touched his chin.

Quietly and patiently Dam listened to the conversations. People were talking about their overseas trips and one fellow had wrestled an alligator in Africa. Another fellow had dressed up as a gorilla and lived with them for seven years. That story brought smiles all round. Dam was about to tell them that he communicated with crocodiles and how he used to take one to school each day in his suitcase to help the foreign language teachers learn some Australian swear words.

Presently the first course was placed under his nose. It was soup and had little red flecks in it that looked like flecks of nail varnish. He looked across at Mary's hands which were now ungloved. They were old and gnarled like crocodiles and their red nails were as long as sabres.

Dam waited until the others began to pick up the appropriate spoon and begin eating. He picked up his spoon; it was huge how the hell was he going to fit it all in his mouth? He watched as Henry delicately tipped the spoon and ladled the nail clippings in. Dam paddled the soup around a little and gathered a considerable spoonful and brought it towards his quivering lips.

"Do enjoy your soup" said Death, "you must eat it all. I won't tell you what's in it, that's for you to guess."

Dam burnt his lips badly. Goodness it was damn hot! His face melted when the spoon came close and he broke out into a sweat. Dam wondered how these people could eat this flaming hot stuff so quickly. He sat there a while sucking his bottom lip and twisting and untwisting his legs under the table. He blew on his spoon fiercely. Death stopped eating and smiled at him deliciously before the metal of her spoon clanged on her delicate teeth.

Half way through the meal Dam's toupee fell in his soup. Aghast he stared at it slowly sinking in the finger nail soup which immediately turned black. Dam stirred it in and watched the broom hairs fall out. What would the dead man think now if he knew his burnt hair was drowning in boiling soup complete with nail clippings, boot polish, poisonous glue, and horse hair from a broom?

The hairs rose and fell and gradually came apart. Now Dam was thinking about the poor horse.

"Come on Damuall, next course is not coming until you've eaten all your soup."

"But..."

"Sorry no buts" she said winking at him. "It came out of a very expensive packet."

Dam was itemising to himself, the cost of each hair on the toupee and was going to say also that the soup was overwhelmingly rich.

Remembering his manners he sat up stiff backed and correct, his soup spoon flaying to create wind above the steaming brew, occasionally dipping in to stir the spoil, plunging under to the depths of his despair. He wondered if he'd find a finger.

He fashioned his lips and took a mighty gulp.

"Um," he mused, "tastes better" he said to himself, "cooled down too!"

Apparently nobody noticed that his toupee had gone and he had a black patch on his forehead and his nose had a black streak down to its tip.

They were so old they were all blind he thought, at least the shoe polish was black what luck he thought. Dam finished his soup gallantly. It didn't taste too bad after all and the toupee, though a little chewy was delicately flavoured. Dam looked at Death and smiled.

"Was it dried fish?" he asked.

"No, no darling," she replied "but you wait until you see the next course!" Dam belched toupee residue, horse hairs and boot polish. The conversation rattled around the table like the gastronomic pulsations of something being digested. Dam began to feel a little hazy and the laughter and voices turned into a wind.

Presently the next course came out on a large plate. It was a huge lobster not one but six of them! The largest one mounted itself in front of Dam and watched Dam watching it.

Suddenly Dam saw it move and fearing that it might disrupt the table he leapt to his feet, flaring his nostrils and bashed it with his stick not once but three times!

When he was convinced it was dead he sat back down and looked at Death. To his surprise she had moved and was sitting a lot further away from him holding her chest with her mouth open.

Dam was the first to speak "What are you doing way down there?"

But then she came horribly close, in fact Dam could practically read the label on the soup packet. Dam spoke again "You've got to watch them!" he said belching glue and boot polish. "You can boil them for weeks but they will still be alive!"

There was stunned silence as he continued, "I remember (burp) when I was in (burp) Ramradddderisdickle in the North (burp) and the local lads (burp) caught one of these (burp) and they boiled it for (burp) two days and when it came to the hotel it had hold of the taxi driver by the (burp) throat. Luckily I had my shot-gun and I blasted the (burp) stuffing outa it 'n' we found one of its legs up a palm tree and (burp) we feasted off it for weeks!" he said as he flared his nostrils and took a massive intake of air.

Stunned silence. Dam leaned forward and picked up a lobster leg saying "This one's a tiddler; mind you they've got claws like vice grips." Dam settled back a little remembering his manners. Everybody believed he was a little drunk.

"Thank you Damuall," said Death at last. Catching her breath. "Why it might have eaten us!" she squeaked.

"I'll check the others," said Dam striding around the table with his stick in the air. One old man said,

"Nonsense" and reached across to break a leg off with his hand. Quick as a flash Dam poked him in the chest with his stick, the fellow gasped and fell back wheezing into his chair.

"Be careful," said Dam as he prodded it with his stick.

When he was satisfied that the others were dead he limped back to his chair. He was about to sit down when he noticed another one's eyes move! He raised his stick and was about to strike when it screamed. Belching and bending down closer to have as look, he soon realised it had human features and was not a lobster after all.

"Oh I do beg your pardon!" he said in his most perfect English. He sat down politely and pulled a napkin around his neck, wiping his brow and blowing his nose with it. He looked at the napkin, it was black!

"Are you alright Damuall?" asked Death and added "here have some water."

"I'm fine thank you" said Dam belching glue and boot polish. He reached in to the middle of the table and with both hands tore a leg off the smashed up lobster. This is going to be fun he said to himself using his hands with his elbows on the table.

Dam ate shell and all. His loud crunching sound could be heard in the kitchen and people stood at the doorway and watched. Juices squirted everywhere with every bite and Mary's face became badly streaked as though she'd been crying. Death was fidgeting with the shell trying to entice the meat out with knife and fork. Dam came to her rescue and miraculously produced a large pair of pliers which he used to crush her legs with.

"Any other legs need crushing? Remember no other course until you've had your legs crushed!" he shouted snapping the pliers together in the air. Everybody said "Yes" so Dam spent an awful lot of time belching and crushing up legs.

"Oh dear me! Thank goodness for you!" said Death as she battered her eyelids and smiled at Dam.

Suddenly there was a loud explosion from down the corridor in the vicinity of the broom cupboard. And the stuffy butler came hurtling into the room covered in flames. The men stood up and the women shrieked. Mary's hair flew up in the air and fell on the table. Dam quickly whisked the table cloth off the table so rapidly that nothing moved on the top of it. And tackled the flaming butler with it, wrapping him up like a spider with a fly. Next he produced a fire extinguisher from his coat and charged down the hall way.

Death was ringing the fire brigade when Dam returned and said the fire was out and asked for desert. Fortunately the butler was not badly burnt and Dam administered some strange cream from a tube he miraculously produced.

He then tore up some of his sheet and wrapped the burns with ice.

Death looked pale she was slumped in a chair watching Dam, her hair somewhat in disarray. She was sort of frothing bubbles and looked the colour of cooked lobster.

Guests began leaving and Dam stood at the top of the stairs and shook all their hands.

"So nice to meet you!" he said to them as they descended.

Death stirred and spoke, "Oh the desert!"

"Desert!" echoed Dam loudly, "I'll stay for dessert!"

There were several people left including Mary and Henry and Death asked Dam if he would get the desert from the kitchen. Dam hobbled down the hall with his stick and presently came back with a huge pavlova the size of a baby's bath. Dam's tummy began to rumble you could hear all the lobster shell grinding into each other like gravel in a cement mixer.

Dam set it down amongst the dead lobsters and the other debris on the table. He was about to serve some, ladies first of course when there was an unexpected black out.

"Not to worry" said Dam as he produced his lighter which he lit and put in the middle of the table. Mary looked at Henry and Henry looked at Dam who was serving pavlova and putting it in soup bowls with soup spoons while Death stared at the lighter then looked at them all.

She was transfixed by the flame! Dam gobbled his pavlova so grossly it collected in globules of froth about his chin. Henry and Mary sat silently along with the game few barely able to eat. Dam helped himself to three helpings and after each serve kept belching toupee residue and said,

"Come on Dirthy dear, you don't know what you're missing out on, no next course until you've finished this one, ha ha ha ha!"

Death winced, she was alive. Mary and Henry rose to leave along with the rest. Dam raced to the door.

"So nice to meet you" he said shaking all their hands. When Henry produced his hand Dam crushed it with his pliers. Mary tried to avoid shaking hands with Dam but he snatched it up and kissed it and said while belching glue and boot-polish,

"I wish you many holes in one." Dam limped back to the glow of the cigarette lighter.

The members of the music group had gone so Dam forgetting to wipe his face disappeared and left Death still staring at the flame.

Then through the black smokey stillness of the house, 'Home, Home On the Range' came belting out of the piano. It was one of Dam's favourites and then he began to sing.

Loud groaning noises came from the cocooned butler who lay on the couch in the same room. Dam stopped playing and limped back towards the light.

She was still there half smiling. Dam took his radio out and turned it up. It was playing rock and roll.

"Ooh!" may I have the pleasure" he said stepping lightly forward, bowing low and holding out his hand to her. She did not move, the flame kept her eye. Dam plied her limp hand off the table and beckoned her to rise.

She rose like a rose and he swept her into his arms belching glue.

At first he held her close, so close the pavlova smeared all over her powdered soft cheek. Gradually Dam's limp improved and he began to let himself go a little.

God he hadn't felt this young in years! His legs were going mad. Death let herself be spun round and round her tight dress made her look like a young ostrich. In the half glow of the lighter she looked adorable and Dam's enthusiasm knew no bounds. With a high pitched squeal of excitement he gave her an almighty spin and she skidded across the floor and smashed through a tall window and fell outside in the garden.

"Oh no!" cried Dam as he raced to the verge and peered out into the cold.

He couldn't see a thing and there was not movement. He leapt out and found her with his feet and then with his hands to ascertain which way her body lay.

He bent down and picked her up then dropped her as she was so heavy.

Too heavy to lift in through the window. He began to drag her. First by the arms, that was no good her neck was too long and her head kept stopping on things. So he bent his little scrawny body and took both her ankles and took off towards the front door. That was no good either as there were too many obstacles in the way.

Finally in pitch black he had her in his arms even though she was a little limp. With great difficulty he carried and half dragged her body towards the front door. However he collided straight into a rose bush. He was badly cut and pierced. He dropped her and began to feel his way. With hands outstretched he felt another and another rose bush.

"Of all the places in the world to find oneself in in the middle of the night!" he thought. He went back to where he thought she was but couldn't find her.

He found her by falling over her, at last united again. He struggled forward through the thorns never wincing as their clothes, especially hers, were torn and shredded as they went. After he had travelled what seemed like hours he realised he'd gone the wrong way so he gave up and threw her over his shoulders and started back the other way! When he finally reached the front door he had carried Death until he was exhausted.

He staggered up to the front door, carried her into the large room and was about to lie her gently on the floor when he found he could not lower her off his shoulders that easily. He fell upon his knees; the sheer volume of her dragged him down until he was lying with his nose squashed into the expensive carpet. Death was upon him and he was pinned to the floor! He suddenly felt terribly depressed; perhaps it was the thought of all that soup and other food above. With a great effort he crawled out and came up for air. He then fetched his cigarette lighter and came hurriedly back to inspect her for any wounds.

He bent over her and turned the gas up. Immediately a bolt of flame a meter long roared into the air. The Butler groaned again and Death's eyes flickered from the past. At least she was still alive and not bleeding.…. much.

Dam looked at his own arms and legs and found he had blood and cuts everywhere.

Dam stood up still panting. Maybe it was time to go. He hobbled over to retrieve his coat and came back with some curtains as well which he'd found on the walls. These he spread out over Death.

He bent down close still belching uncontrollably. She groaned - at least she was still breathing.

Dam found his stick and coat and was soon in his little blue car driving home. He thought often about Death as he drove and when he arrived home he found he'd mistakenly put three brass forks and three soup spoons, three copper ash trays in one pocket and in another pocket he found to his great surprise a brass candle holder, two brass door knobs, three surveryettes rings and a can of boot polish submerged in what looked like pavlova.

He felt embarrassed about that and often said it would be good manners to take it all back one day. But damn it all for some reason he never did. He let his hair grow and his beard grow long again. He was too busy with his own life to think again about Death.

Dam goes to the Museum

Normally Dam was a chirpy kind of person. Always standing either on his toes or his heels, never needing to grip a support. This day he was standing flat-footed, deep in thought as he'd found an interesting stone in his backyard when he was playing golf with a large wooden driver he'd made from the root of an iron-bark tree which he'd dug out of the ground some years earlier. The day he'd dug it out he'd found many stones and had put them in a small pile. As he was playing golf and hitting the stones rather than golf balls, he noticed one stone was different from the others.

He picked it up and examined it. Turning it about in his hand where it suddenly fitted perfectly. He noticed that the exposed edge was very sharp.

To Dam it looked like a prehistoric tool for it fitted in his hand in such a way that it turned into a comfortable cutting or scraping implement.

Dam was off to the museum. He'd heard about the new building they were constructing and decided he'd like to visit and see if they could help him identify his new stone. Dam's old car rattled along and the stone bounced on the floor beside him. On the way he stopped at the laundry as he had to pick up his mother's crocodile skin hat which she had used to stop herself from being scalped when she practised her archery. As an innovator his mother had designed and made a special kind of bow to fire bent sticks called boomerangs.

The boomerangs returned automatically if they missed their target.

It was a cold day so he put the tight fitting cap on. She had left two spines on the top of it which looked like horns.

When he arrived at the museum he was told to go and see professor Mudlump for he was the expert on identifying prehistoric tools.

Dam listened intently to the directions to professor Mudlump's room and went off clutching his stone tightly in his hand. Down two flights of stairs he went then right, then left and right before you, if you make it that far and right again if you have any energy left!

Dam was soon lost. There were rooms everywhere some of these were full of exhibits in tall cases which Dam spent quite a few hours studying.

Presently somebody came by and Dam asked them where the professor's room was.

"Up three flights of stairs, down the corridor to the right, past the elephants and the chimpanzees and you can't miss him, he's been there for years."

Dam walked on, he wished he could fly, his legs were not used to all the stairs and the flat ground. He passed room after room. He went inside one room out of curiosity and found a whole lot of Dinosaur fossils with feathers all over them! In another room he found some huge turtle shells with rocks in their stomachs. And still more birds with rocks in their stomachs! Dam thought they had to eat rocks to stay on the ground. He put his hand in his pocket and felt his stone tool and kept walking.

Suddenly and without any warning the lights went out. He stopped still, it was totally black and quite cold. He couldn't hear any sound.

He sat down and waited for the blackout to clear but it didn't. As he sat there he was sure he could hear bats flying past him and even feel the wind from their wings. He could smell them too! They smelt like something very old.

"How nice it would be to fly" he said to himself as he sniffed the cold air.

Presently someone came bumbling along in the dark.

"Excuse me," said Dam. There was a great crash as the person had obviously received a shock.

"Whose there?" came a gravelly voice.

"It's a blackout" said Dam. Then, not feeling much like a blackout he added,

"I was looking for professor Mudlump's room."

"Ah!" cried the man "I am professor Mudlump, what can I do for you?"

"I have a stone here I would like you to identify." Dam reached out in the dark in the direction of the professor's voice. He touched the professor on the hand and noticed he felt cold and damp. The professor took the stone.

"Oh yes, this is definitely an early piece," he said as he instinctively gripped the stone the right way.

"How old would it be?" asked Dam.

"Oh, much older than you and I put together." Dam reckoned that would be rather old as he had lost count of his own age some centuries before! Something inside Dam wanted him to be as old as the stone.

"You hang onto this, young man," said the professor returning the stone, "you may need it and I will try to find a way out. They've been building underground and when we get blackouts they go on for a lifetime and if you don't know your way around you'll get lost - follow me."

As Dam began to follow he felt a sudden pain below his knee and stumbled. Moments after the professor let out a loud scream and seemed to fall into a very black hole. After a horrible length of time Dam heard him hit water!

"Are you alright?" Dam yelled as he crawled to the black space and felt it with his hand. There wasn't any reply. Only an empty blackness and a cold breeze.

Dam smelt the air, it was very muddy. He turned around on all fours and began to crawl slowly. After all he was Dam Diligent and he could see in the dark. He blinked and banged the side of his head with his hand and all of a sudden he could see bright flashes of coloured lights. But they soon faded and left him staring in the dark.

He crawled on a bit further then with a great effort stood up and gingerly took a step. After a while he noticed a little pale glow and was able to walk but he felt uncomfortable and began to look for walls and objects to hold on to.

Dam walked on his heels and toes and for the first time in his life he felt he needed a support.

He was surrounded by boxes with stuffed animals in them. Then bones and more birds. He began to think of his rock and he took it out of his pocket.

Suddenly, bang! He crashed into something with a sharp edge. His legs went from under him as though time had swept him away and he fell into whatever it was! It turned out to be a knee-high vat of glue! He had damaged his knee for he'd fallen in head first! The glue had covered his arms and face and legs, a very sticky mess! He climbed out but soon climbed back in as he'd dropt his rock and he wasn't going to lose that! With his rock in hand he climbed out again thoroughly saturated. He changed direction and while rubbing his eyes he slipped on the glue and fell into a black space, his feet no longer in contact with the floor. Something had caught him by one leg and held him upside down suspended in mid-air!

He felt his leg, it was caught and entangled in rope. Dam struggled to be free but soon stopped as he wondered what was below him, thinking of the professor's fate or maybe even worse! He hung there upside down, drying for a little while as he wiped his eyes.

He reached up and caught the rope. It was tight and difficult to undo.

Luckily he had his stone knife and soon began to cut through it until he was hanging by a thread.

"If I fall I shall flap my arms hard if I can't grip the rope," he said.

Dam fell. He flapped his arms furiously. But it was no use. It was the glue which had closed his hand around the stone and weighed him down.

Dam he fell not too far, however he landed on something hard and dislocated his jaw! Fortunately he'd landed in something very soft. It smelt like a colony of bats! However it turned out to be a large box of feathers and hair! As Dam stood up he found he had somehow damaged his knee. He tried to close his jaw but couldn't nor could he straighten his leg. He let out an "oorgawank" sound as he tried to walk and groaned.

Growling now with pain his eyelids were gummed up with feathers and his jaw was stretched to its horrible maximum. He scraped at his eyelids with the sharp stone. He couldn't see anything without putting his head well back so he stopped scraping after awhile. At least the feathers weren't white he could just see that!

Staring and blinking, undeterred he crawled along, first on one leg then like a one legged mouse on his toes. But his knee was terribly painful. So he crawled along upside down backwards on two hands and one leg! His extended jaw would not close. After crawling up two flights of stairs in the dark and many corners he came to a grizzly halt. He realised he was cold and hungry and not getting anywhere. His knee was not getting better.

Groaning and growling he crawled into a little round ball and went to sleep. After a short time he woke up in agony as pins and needles were shooting about in his good leg and these were making his jaw try to close. He changed position and changed position again he was cold and uncomfortable.

Dam tossed and turned and woke up many times in the night and the last time he woke he found himself surrounded by flashing lights! He tried to speak but all that came out was a roar and a growl. Completely dazed he could hear people's voices in the glaring light.

Dam's knee loosened and his jaws let go of his knee which he found himself chewing. Immediately his hands fell as if from nowhere and he collapsed on the ground. He realised then he'd been asleep on one leg with his arms supported above his head. Looking around he found himself in a little display booth and the crowd which had gathered around were pointing cameras at him and laughing.

"Where are you from?" they asked. "Are you a dinosaur?" Dam let out a loud roar, groaned and finished with "Gondwana!" He raised his arms in the air like a madman.

The people laughed though some backed away. Dam stood up making peculiar noises and banged on the glass with his stone and the glass cracked and broke. The people screamed and quickly ran away. He stepped down and tried to straighten himself. His jaw would not close and he was ten centimetres larger all around with feathers and hair! "Professor Mudlump indeed," he thought.

A man approached him and half blinded him for no reason at all with a flash bulb.

The museum looked totally different in the light. He noticed he was in the feathered dinosaur section.

With a sore jaw and a sore knee he limped off down the corridor. He had not gone far when he came to a door which read, "Professor Mudlump."

"I wonder if this is the place?" he said to himself. He tapped on the door and it immediately opened and out from inside came a long black claw which gripped Dam by the throat and drew him hastily forward. Dam let out a cry, yelling,

"Goannadorkwalk!" and attacked it with his stone tool. In a flurry of feathers he tore the arm off the creature. It was made of feathers, hair and wood and belonged to Professor Mudlump. It was his personal remote controlled dinosaur! There was a loud laughing sound from inside the room and a smiling professor greeted Dam as he stood on one leg above the wreck of the dinosaur.

"Ah, ha, ha, what millennium are you from?" the professor asked reaching out his hand to Dam who was still quite agitated and distressed.

"An gawak goink," is all that came out of his mouth. He was shocked at himself, he was meant to say,

"I'm so pleased to meet you again."

"An gowalk ga wok!" there it was again! Was it really Dam who was saying that?

The professor ushered him in so Dam limped cautiously towards a chair.

"Lum doric um oowa alls up," Professor Mudlump looked at Dam and frowned saying,

"Do you really think we'd say you had not survived?"

Dam sat down and held out his rock. With the other hand he prized each finger off it and gave it to the professor. Dam took off his shirt as he was so hot and began pulling feathers from it and dusting it.

The professor looked shocked. Dam wondered if he thought he was shedding his skin?

"Ahhrgh um olist oo!" said Dam with his jaw still open. "What on earth did that mean?" he said to himself. He gripped his jaw and tried to move it up and down. The professor laughed as though he completely understood and left with Dam's shirt. Perhaps he was going to put it in a box thought Dam. He sat down and examined his sore knee. It looked like it had teeth marks around it. When the professor returned Dam said, "Uggunks."

The professor handed back his washed shirt, though it was a little damp and said,

"If you go down to the laundry on the third floor they will dry it for you. Oh, Professor Mudlumps was my predecessor. He mysteriously disappeared twenty five years ago, some say he haunts the building at night. They reckon he eats old exhibits, ha ha!"

Dam scratched his leg, his knee felt sore as though somebody had taken a lump of flesh from it.

"Here take your rock," said the professor.

"Plt olt oo," said Dam.

"It's chert," said the professor, "a type of stone,"

"Ank oo," said Dam as he limped over the dead dinosaur in the doorway and out into the hallway.

He turned and went down the stairs plucking the feathers from his chin and pants.

He found the laundry by accident as he was nearly run over by a large trolley of steaming dinosaur skins. The gentleman pushing it simply called out, "Laundry!"

Dam went inside. The room was full of steam. People in robes with funny animal skin hats on were stirring great steaming vats. There was the sound of running water in the background. Dam walked into the steam. Presently he came to a small bench beside what looked like a large heated pool and sat down. He dangled his sore leg over the side and wiggled his toes. With nobody around he decided to go for a swim. He dived in and swam straight to the bottom.

It was crystal clear and he noticed a large fish close to the bottom and then a huge turtle swam towards him. Dam's jaw suddenly snapped back into place and then on the bottom of the pool Dam saw a very old man.

He quickly swam down to him and said, "Mudlumps!"

"Oh, you again, hello!" said the man, "it took you a long time to find me. I was just having a nap!" Mudlumps did not look well and since he'd fallen asleep again Dam took him in his arms and swam back up to the surface. He rested him on the edge of the pool and felt his pulse. There was none. He dragged him over to the laundry door and left him outside then went off to look for an ambulance. Dam was soon lost and only by accident came once again to the laundry door.

Mudlumps had disappeared. Dam set about walking on his heels and then on his toes.

He wasn't having such a bad time after all. He was properly dressed, nice and warm, pants nice and clean and a nice clean shirt. The museum wasn't such a bad place after all and he still had his rock in his pocket. At least he'd found out a few things about his rock. He tried to remember what the person had said about it. He said it was old and held in such a way and…. well he'd forgotten the rest.

Dam decided to take the lift to the top of the building that way he could go around all the floors and not miss ground level.

As he was going round and around he came upon an upright display case with the words "Mudlumps, Second century B.C. Found in an ancient Sumerian laundry" written on it.

He looked like he'd been fossilized! How long had Dam been going around and around the museum for! He looked at his hands.

Finally the day came when he found his way out. He hobbled down the stairs into the sunshine and looked for his little old car but it was gone!

Something suddenly shot past him at a tremendous speed. It was shaped like a boomerang! Then another and another. Dam felt his head for his crocodile skin hat, it had gone. Soon he realised that there were human beings sitting in the middle of these boomerangs! They all had large black eyes and looked at Dam as they passed.

There weren't any cars anywhere and the city was immense with huge buildings which disappeared into the sky!

Dam walked towards his home; but which way was that? Everything had changed. He had lost time! He walked around in a large circle before he realised there was no going back.

Though one thing had not changed. He put his hand in his pocket and grasped the stone. It was no longer a stone, it was once again a useful tool. Dam tip-toed back up the steps and disappeared back into the museum.

Dam Grows a Kidney

Early one morning Dam went to the fridge to look for food. He'd forgotten to look in the garden for food so he stood at the fridge and barely found anything to eat. He was hungry, he was poor. He went over to the sink and drank half a glass of water and nearly choked on it. He sat down and glanced at the paper noticing an advertisement offering five thousand dollars for a kidney. He sat up; he could eat well on five thousand dollars he said. He looked at the advertisement to find out what sort of kidney they meant because there are lots of different kidneys such as kidney beans…

"Human kidneys!" he said out loud. He felt uneasy a small pain in his lower back.

"Donate your kidney and save another person's life" it said. He sat back five thousand dollars for doing nothing isn't bad he thought. He pulled some chocolate from out of his pocket and took a bite. "I'll grow my kidney healthy!" he said to himself. He stood up slowly like an old man, his knees cracked and he moaned. His back was sore. He decided to go on a diet to ensure that his kidneys were okay. First of all he began to drink a lot of water. He sat in his kitchen and drank four glasses of water every hour for sixteen days. He then went out into his backyard and picked many strange plants and herbs which he put in the sink and began to squash with his feet. He drank the juice every now and again after adding a lot of sugar.

When he felt his kidneys were well he went along to the horse-piddle (hospital) to sell one and save another person's life! "Thank you, Mr Diligent," said the lady behind the counter. The docked-door (which was

Dam's word for "doctor" as they always seemed to be chopping up openings) gave Dam a cheque for five thousand dollars.

"Your kidney seems to be in good shape," the docked-door said. Dam left, he was down a kidney, he didn't feel any heavier on one side. He felt fine.

He stopped by at the shops and bought lots of ice-cream and cream and milk, huge lumps of black sugar and chocolate. After all real food came from shops he said.

Next day when he was eating breakfast the phone rang. They'd found something wrong with his kidney and since they couldn't use it, did he want it back? Dam finished his ice-cream and said he'd better come and get it as he didn't want it to die. He was given his kidney in a glass jar. It looked cold and alone. Dam took it home and spoke to it. He asked it if it was hungry then realised he was hungry himself and that since it was his kidney it would be hungry too. He went and squashed some special plants and herbs and added them to the water in the jar. Straight away the kidney sat up and began to shiver then bounce from side to side.

"Ah it's feeding" said Dam.

As the days passed Dam would wake when his kidney woke and slept when it slept. After sometime it seemed to outgrow the jar so he bought a larger one and put it in that. But it even out-grew that jar so he put it in a bucket! Dam began to look puzzled. The less food he gave it the bigger it grew. It began to grow immense. At feeding time it would shake and wobble and create waves.

It became so large he had to put it in the bath! He was kept busy all day carrying buckets in and out of his bathroom.

The kidney still seemed to eat a lot and still seemed to be growing. Dam only had to go near it and it would rear up to look at him and begin to wobble, expecting food.

Life seemed a lot more difficult with an external kidney waiting to be fed in the bath.

Dam thought the size of it would surely raise the price.

"Must be worth a fortune now!" he'd say as he rolled it over to ensure it didn't develop bath sores.

Finally the day arrived when he decided to take it back and see if he could sell it.

He gripped it with both arms as he found it was extremely heavy and somehow managed to roll it up the side of the bath and into a wheel-barrow.

He then filled the wheel-barrow with water and began walking down the street sloshing a little water here and there.

Dam arrived at Casually, which was his name for "Casualty" because they always seemed to take so long to do things at horse-piddle, with his giant kidney in a wheel-barrow.

The woman behind the counter was speechless and ran out to find a docked-door. The docked-door quickly ordered Dam down the corridor and into a room.

"This kidney has a disease!" said the docked-door rather hastily. "A rare blood disorder. It must be destroyed and you must be vaccinated."

"Oh," said Dam and added "But how will you destroy my kidney." The docked-door then administered several potions to the water and left the room.

Dam looked at his kidney in the wheel-barrow. It seemed to be sleeping. "Poor kidney," he said to it.

Meanwhile Dam was vaccinated, he didn't really understand why and the needles kept breaking off in his arm!

The docked-door came back with many people and while they were huddled around Dam's kidney a loud shot rang out. But the bullet seemed to ricochet and miss, then another and another.

Dam heard one of them say it was full of stones. Then all the docked-doors jumped on it and began to strangle it. A massive struggle ensued and it was sometime before things quietened down.

Dam rushed in and found his kidney dying before his eyes.

"This kind of disease makes kidneys believe they have a mind, which of course is nonsense, that's why we have to destroy them," said the docked door.

Dam pushed his wheel-barrow full of rocks back home. Next time he was going to sell a body organ he'd better do better than that he said to himself kicking the ground and stubbing his toe.

"Ouch!" he said holding his toe, then added, "I wonder how much they'd give me for my foot?"

Dam Diligent Takes a Break

Dam had been mowing lawns for a living and feeding himself, not with the grass he cut but with various foodstuffs he bought from the local shop which he visited often.

He hated visiting the shop and spending money but worst of all there was a woman serving there who was difficult to stop talking once she started. "Excuse me I have to go," Dam said on a number of occasions. The woman replied,

"I don't waste your time like you waste your money…buying chocolates at your age!" How did she know how old he was anyway? Dam fixed her with his one hundred and twenty year old stare, smirked and walked out.

"Maybe she is right?" he thought as he drove home in his little blue car.

"Perhaps I need better food like fish to keep me alive longer." Dam hated the thought of growing old like his lawn, then being cut down by time and worse put in a box to rot in the ground and not being able to get out and eat chocolate again.

Some time ago Dam had fixed a propeller to the differential of his car and frequently used the car as a boat. It was waterproof and he could listen to the radio as he fished out the window.

He looked at a map and found an island. He decided to motor out to it and have a look and maybe fish somewhere near it. He packed his lunch and found his fishing gear and was soon driving down the beach and out through the waves. The little car bounced through the sea as though it was riding along a country road. The island was not far off shore and soon the car slowed and Dam stuck his head out the window. The sea was deep green and the island's black rocks were girthed in white foam. As Dam watched he noticed a rock platform on the island which he thought he may be able to drive the car along and since he was feeling a little adventurous he decided to motor closer and have a good look. Presently he found himself bumping along the rock platform on the island, the sea only knee deep around the car.

He put his head out the window again and watched the waves drain off the platform into a deep hole.

"Ah," said Dam "there'll be fish down there." He took out his lines and found a very strong one and put two large sinkers on it and a big hook large enough to catch a huge fish.

"I wonder if fish eat chocolate" he said taking a little nibble of the bait.

He was just about to cast it out the window when he heard a loud pop and a fizz. Dam said "damn" as he realised he had a flat tyre. The car sagged to one side at the front and bubbles rose up in the foam. Carefully he put his line down on the seat next to him and turned the radio on, it was playing a waltz.

Humming the tune Dam took his pants off and opened the car door when the wave receded, he was going to change the wheel and he closed the door as the next wave came in. When it receded he opened the boot and reached quickly in for the jack. He closed it just in time as another wave came in. The water was cold and it played mischief around his knees. Quickly he positioned the jack and began to raise the car. When it was raised enough he tried to undo the nuts but the wheel turned as well. So he lowered the car as the wave receded and undid the nuts while the car was on the ground then raised it again as the wave came in.

In no time at all he had the spare tyre on the car and the flat one in the boot. He felt around for the wheel nuts and couldn't find them anywhere; the waves had washed them away. Not to worry, he said as he took some nuts off the other front wheel and put them on the new wheel. He was soon back in his car ready to throw his line out.

He put his arm out the car window and spun the line round and round, faster and faster then let go. But the line missed the deep water falling just short of the deep hole.

He tried to wind he line in but the hook had caught on a piece of rubbery sea-weed and was stuck. Dam pulled and pulled but the line did not come. He wound up the line as tight as it would go and gripped the reel. With a mighty pull he managed to free the hook however the line with the two large sinkers came shooting back at him with such force that they hit him in the forehead, one above each eye with a double, bang, bang!

Dam dropt the line and let out a loud cry as he gripped his forehead.

He looked at himself in the rear vision mirror and two large red holes began to bleed. He felt for a rag under the seat and wrapped his head in it.

"Lucky I'm not blind" he said as he took a big bite off his chocolate-bait-lunch.

He turned the radio off as it was playing a happy tune and he felt awfully miserable. He was wet and cold and his head felt like he'd been shot twice.

"I hate fishing" he said to himself, "something always goes wrong!"

He ate more chocolate and looked out the window. He started the windscreen wipers as the salt had encrusted on the glass as he could not see. He noticed a large dark cloud on the horizon with storm clouds brewing. It was then that he decided to forget about fishing and drive home.

He started the car and chose the right moment to drive off the platform into a wave. The car splashed under the wave, temporally submerging and bobbed to the surface again. He was on his way home. The windscreen wipers were thrashing furiously and Dam was chewing chocolate. He turned the radio back on, it was playing a waltz so Dam began to hum.

Suddenly without warning the car began to vibrate as though something had caught in the propeller. He gripped the wheel biting his tongue at the same time. The vibrations became worse then much to Dam's despair the car began to sink! He revved the engine and leaned forward his eyes on the approaching shoreline.

He looked in the rear vision mirror and saw two objects floating behind him. As he looked harder he realised they were his wheels!

He tried to turn around but had little steerage as the two wheels were off the front. He worked the steering wheel into full lock and gradually managed to come alongside one of the wheels. It bumped into his door. He wound the window down and began climbing up onto the roof of the car. When he was half way out headfirst he realised he couldn't continue as there was nothing to hold on to on the roof. He had to climb back in and come out legs first then stand on the runner board before he could hoist himself up on the roof. Fortunately it was one of those rare fishing expeditions when he had actually remembered to bring the anchor. He had strapped it to the front of his car before he left.

Now he found himself opening his eyes under water trying to untie the knots which held it to the front bumper bar. Eventually he threw the anchor out and caught the wheel and pulled it up onto the roof. With the weight of the extra tyre the car sank lower in the water. He secured the tyre to the roof using the anchor hooked in the passenger window with the rope going through the opposite window and up to the wheel. Then he climbed back down into the car head first through his window. A little water had splashed into the car so his feet were now submerged on the accelerator pedal. Dam sat up and scanned the horizon for the other wheel. It was no good it had disappeared.

With the back wheels still in place and spinning and the propeller still propelling, Dam sped ever closer to the shoreline, though steering without the front wheels was very awkward. As he was nearing the shoreline the level of the sea began to lap the windscreen and because the anchor rope ran through the two front windows which were open slightly open, water began to squirt in at him. One jet came at him from his left side the other from his right. He reached his hands up to stop them both and the steering wheel went out of control. Dam grabbed the wheel and the water squirted in on him.

Suddenly the steering wheel spun left then right, it was doing peculiar things, the car was out of control. Then all at once the steering wheel came right off in his hands! Dam looked around for the nuts which held it on and could only find one sloshing around in the bottom of his car. He struggled to put the wheel back on as the water was squirting in his face. Dam looked out the window to see where he was going. Still the waltz was playing and the wind-screen wipers were swaying in time. The water was half way up the wind-screen and the wipers were useless.

Then Dam realised the car was sinking. He quickly grabbed some loose anchor rope which was hanging off the roof and looped it around his neck and tied one end to the side of the steering wheel then back around his waist.

As he was tying the knot around his waist he noticed the other steering wheel nut on the floor washing about. Without thinking he snatched it up and tried to put it back on the bolt but it was too difficult so he threaded it onto the rope.

Then with one foot on the accelerator he knelt on the seat and pushed his stomach forward so that the steering wheel found the bolts on the steering column and with his arms outstretched his hands stopped the leaks from the windows as best they could. Dam manoeuvred his body to steer the car and fortunately for him the shore was only meters away. Soon the water became shallower and receded and he could bring his hands together about the wheel.

Finally he drove up onto the pebbly beach. The car was tilting forward steeply but he only wanted to get home!

He searched for the plug in the bottom of the car to drain all the water out. There were all sorts of things floating about in the car. There was his lunch, some rope, carpets, fishing lines, maps, pieces of wood, more rags, empty ice-cream containers, an old esky, quite a few books, towels, blankets, pillows, shoes, to name a few. The plug hole began screaming loudly as all the debris began to circle above it.

Dam did not like to waste time for apart from money, time was the worst thing to waste. He began driving with no front wheels grinding over the rocks and leaving a trail of water as the plug hole let out a wailing cry.

At last he was driving along the road and after going some distance he remembered he had a wheel on the roof and a flat tyre in the boot. He stopped the car and with some difficulty emerged from it with the steering wheel still tied around his stomach and the rope looped around his neck and waist.

He untied the anchor from the wheel on the roof and jacked up the car. But alas there were no nuts to keep the wheels on. He went to the rear wheels and found three which could be spared so he put two on the good wheel and one on the flat wheel.

Dam was an expert at knots however this time when he went to get back in the car he found he was somewhat tangled not only with anchor rope but with fishing line as well. Eventually in desperation and to save time he hurled some of it in the boot with the jack and some of it in through the window. Then he squeezed in and sat down.

Dam let out a loud shriek and nearly launched himself through the windscreen for he had sat on a fish hook!

"Not another one!" he exclaimed. He tried wriggling it out of his bottom but he was hooked firmly. He resumed driving by kneeling on the seat with his right knee while twisting his left leg around out in front and pressing on the accelerator.

The car had a horrible lean and a jerk to it with the two front wheels not quite right but at least he could go a little faster. Not far down the road as he was turning a corner, the car veered to the left then slammed back to the middle of the road and the wheel with the flat tyre shot off over an embankment.

He stopped. The emptying water let out a final scream so Dam turned the radio on to drown out the sound. He emerged again from his car with the fish hook in his bottom and the steering wheel tied to his stomach with the nuts attached trailing anchor rope and fishing line. He stood at the top of the embankment and spied the wheel forty feet below.

"I may get down but I'll never get back up" he said as he climbed back into his car. Steering the car with only one front wheel was extremely difficult, he had two hands but his stomach kept getting in the way. He tried to put the nuts back on the steering column but there was no way he could tighten them. He left them hanging on the rope. Over one more hill and his grinding wheel hub and loud music could be heard from kilometres around.

The shop came into view and Dam thought he'd like some chocolate for dinner. The thought of fish did not appeal to him at all not even if it meant a longer life. As he was going down the hill to the shop the car crunched forward and the other front wheel became disconnected and raced on ahead of him.

Dam stopped the car again and shuffled about the road, hopelessly lashed to his car, looking for the wheel nuts. Luckily he found them and threaded them onto his never ending neckless of rope.

He clattered forward towards the shop where he stopped the car and turned the radio off. He emerged but found he could only walk a short way as he was so entangled like a spider enmeshed in its own web.

"Help!" he cried hoping the lady would hear him. "Oh please may I have some chocolate?" She came out and stood on the steps above him. He looked pathetic. "Oh please may I have some chocolate?" he repeated.

"Good heavens!" said the lady who was an expert at stating the obvious. "You look like you've got an oily blood soaked rag tied about your forehead, two black eyes and no pants on. Is this the new fashion then? All that rope tied about you – and, oh I like the steering wheel tied to your stomach!"

"Yes," said Dam "it's driving me nuts!"

"I tell you this stuff's bad for you" she went on and on as she threw him some chocolate and added, "I'm not coming near you!" As Dam turned the lady spied the fish hook and exclaimed.

"Oh I like the body piercing!" She watched him go. Dam mumbled something about piercing her body...

When finally home Dam set about removing the fish hook. He had been to the horse-piddle (hospital) too much lately. The nurses were well acquainted with "The Flying Fish Fillet" as they called him. So he set about removing the fish hook himself. He went to the fridge and filled a large bowel with ice and lowered himself gently down into it. Next he used his fishing knife and a mirror with a pair of pliers and seemed to waste an awful lot of time getting it out. When he was finally freed of all his shackles and woes he lay in a hot bath and felt the two giant lumps on his forehead; like little horns he thought.

But they weren't nearly as large as the lumps of chocolate Dam had for dinner.

Dam's Perfect Day

Dam sat down again. He'd been sitting down for about five days now, watching the black hill opposite as the light of the day passed over it, watching the cloud puffs blow across the clear blue and watching the new shoots on the trees as they puffed up from the ground.

"If I don't do something soon" he said, "I'll go perfectly mad!" Dam sat back and reflected on what he'd said and the flamboyant use of his word "perfectly."

The word "mad" he was already familiar with, that was easy, it was his name spelt backwards.

"Perfectly means just so wonderfully precisely good," he mused and began dividing the word into its syllables, "per-fec-tly."

"Believe you me" he said "there's nothing like being perfectly perfect!"

He then began thinking about all the things he thought were perfect, like spheres and circles, "But then cubes are perfect?" he curiously asked and answered, "Yes, and trees are perfect... flowers too."

Dam thought for a long time and decided that most things in nature, if not all, were perfect and those things which man had made were in some way not perfect.

He looked out and watched the day passing perfectly. Then he noticed way up on the hill a dying tree.

"Ah" he said "there is something in nature that is not perfect - disease."

He looked closer and saw another sick tree then another and another. Till most of the trees Dam could see were in some way suffering and were not perfect. Then he noticed that everything around him was in a state of disease and decay. He held his stomach, was he sick or just hungry?

As the sun went down and its golden light brushed through the trees, Dam arose from his chair and went inside.

That night before he went to sleep he decided that he'd had a perfectly miserable day.

Dam Writes a Book

One day Dam exploded. He literally came apart at the seams and sat down and began to write. He had so many ideas coming into his mind at once he felt he had to get them down on paper so that maybe later when they were all revealed some common thread would emerge, some reason why his mind was working the way it was.

He sat down with a pencil and a clean sheet of paper and the thoughts began to flow. He wrote all day and deep into the night. He crossed mountains, swam rivers and navigated oceans. There were even romantic scenes and the hope of film and television rights. It wasn't till the early hours of the morning that he retired to bed. "It'll be a best seller, what an idea!" he said. Dam slept like a bottle in the waves, he was so eager to get back to writing.

Late the next day he sprang out of bed and dashed to the table. There was the script alright or was it? Dam looked closer. It seemed to be a big long shopping list! He was horrified. He looked all around even under the table. It was no use it was a big long shopping list!

"Maybe it's in code?" he said as he slowly sat down.